Even if an employer felt an attraction for the hired help, most wouldn't let it show. Mac hadn't let it show all day. But, being half asleep, he had let his guard down. Nine chances out of ten he wouldn't even acknowledge this in the morning.

But what if he did?

What if he liked her?

What if living with him for a month was enough that their barriers broke down?

He already had her stuttering and staring. If he made a pass at her, could she resist him?

And what if she didn't?

No one knew better than Ellie that there were consequences to relationships.

Especially relationships with bosses.

MAID FOR
THE SINGLE DAD

BY
SUSAN MEIER

First published in Great Britain 2010
Harlequin Mills & Boon Limited,
Eton House, 18-24 Paradise Road, Richmond, Surrey TW9 1SR

© Linda Susan Meier 2010

ISBN: 978 0 263 21422 2

Harlequin Mills & Boon policy is to use papers that are natural, renewable and recyclable products and made from wood grown in sustainable forests. The logging and manufacturing process conform to the legal environmental regulations of the country of origin.

Printed and bound in Great Britain
by CPI Antony Rowe, Chippenham, Wiltshire

CHAPTER ONE

ELLIE Swanson had not signed up for this.

Yes, she'd agreed to run Happy Maids while her boss, Liz Harper Nestor, took a well-deserved honeymoon after remarrying her gorgeous ex-husband, Cain. And, yes, she was perfectly capable of supervising the fourteen or so employees on Happy Maids's payroll for the four weeks Liz would be in Paris. But she wasn't authorized to make a change in the company's business plan, as the man across the desk wanted her to.

"I'm a friend of Cain's."

Of course he was. Tall and slender with perfect blue eyes and black hair cut short and businesslike, Mac Carmichael wore his tailored navy blue suit with the casual ease of a man accustomed to handmade suits, fine wines and people taking his orders. Just like Cain.

"And he told me his wife's company was the best in town."

"But we're a weekly cleaning service. We don't place maids in clients' homes."

"You should."

A bead of sweat rolled down Ellie's back. The air-conditioning had broken the day Liz left. But Ellie could handle the heat and humidity of June in Miami. What she couldn't abide was failure. Her first day on the job and already she was turning away a client. An important client. A client who could not only tell Cain that Happy Maids hadn't come through for him; he could also tell all his wealthy friends—the very people Liz would be marketing to when she returned.

Ellie leaned back on the chair, tapping a pencil on the desk blotter. "Explain again what you're looking for."

"My maid quit unexpectedly. I need to hire a temporary replacement while I interview for another one."

"I can send someone to your house a few times a week to clean," she said hopefully.

He shook his head. "I have a daughter and a son. They need breakfast every morning."

"Then I'll be happy to send someone every day at seven."

"Lacy gets up at five."

"Then I'll have someone at four."

"I work some nights."

Ellie gaped at him. "You want the maid to be a nanny too?"

He caught her gaze. His sinfully blue eyes held hers and she fought the urge to swallow as pinpricks of attraction sparkled along her nerve endings.

"And live in."

She gasped. "Live in?"

"I also pay very well."

Ah, the magic words. A victim of domestic violence herself, Liz had gotten involved with A Friend Indeed, a charity that helped women transition out of their abusive homes and into new lives. It was a natural fit that Liz should begin employing the women from A Friend Indeed until they got on their feet. Ellie had actually been the first employee Liz had hired after they met at the charity. The company needed every job—especially the good paying ones—to provide work for all the women who wanted help.

Mac rose from his seat. "Look, if your firm can't handle it, I'll be on my way."

He turned to the door.

Stop him!

She bounced out of her chair. "Wait."

He faced her again. This time she did swallow. His eyes reminded her of the ocean in the dead of summer, calm and deep and perfect blue. His dark hair gleamed in the sunlight pouring in from the window to his right. High cheekbones angled to blissfully full lips, the kind that made most women take a second glance and wonder what it would be like to kiss him. It should have been pure pleasure to look at him. Instead, the scowl on his face caused Ellie to doubt the intuition that guided her life.

"Yes?"

"I—" Why had her intuition told her to stop him? She didn't have anybody who could work as a maid/nanny. Most of Liz's employees had kids of their own and homes to get back to every night. They couldn't live in. And that's what he needed.

"I—um—maybe we can work something out."

His scowl grew even darker. "I don't work things out."

No kidding. She didn't need intuition to tell her that.

"I want someone today."

Don't let him go.

She groaned inwardly, wondering why her sixth sense was so insistent on this. But accustomed to listening to the intuition that had saved her life, she couldn't ignore it.

"I'll do it."

His scowl shifted into a look of confusion. "You?"

"I know I'm behind the desk today, but I'm only filling in for Cain's wife, Liz. She runs the business herself, but this month she's on her honeymoon. I'm more than capable of cooking, cleaning and caring for children."

His eyes held hers for another second or two. Then his gaze dipped from her face to her pretty red dress, and Ellie suddenly regretted her decision to wear something as exposing as the short strapless creation made more for having lunch with friends on a sunny sidewalk café than working in an office. But not having air-conditioning had made the choice for her. How was she supposed to know a client would show up?

He smiled and all the air whooshed out of Ellie's lungs. The temperature in her blood rose to an almost unbearable level. She could have melted where she stood. If this guy lived up north, snowflakes wouldn't stand a chance against that smile.

"We have air-conditioning, so you might want to change into jeans and a T-shirt." He took a business card out of his jacket pocket, scribbled on the back and handed it to her. "That's my home address. I'll meet you there in an hour." Then he turned and walked out the door.

Ellie collapsed on the office chair. Damn it! What had she gotten herself into? Now she not only had all of Liz's work, she also had a full-time job. More than full-time! She had to live in!

With a sigh of frustration at herself, she lifted the receiver of the phone on the desk and quickly dialed the number for Cain's personal assistant, Ava.

"Are you busy?"

"Hey, good morning, Magic. How's your first day going?"

"Abysmally. Don't call me Magic anymore. I think my intuition is on the fritz."

Ava laughed.

"I'm serious. Some guy came in here this morning, de-manding a full-time maid and nanny—someone to live in—and I volunteered to take the job."

"Yourself?"

Angling her elbow on the desk, Ellie cradled her chin on her palm. "Yes."

"Oh, that's so not like you!"

"I know. But he's a friend of Cain's and I worried about disappointing him. My intuition got all jumbled while he was here and before I knew it I was taking the job myself." She winced. "I was thinking maybe you could find an agency that can get him a real temporary maid, then call him back and tell him I made a mistake."

"All right. I'll handle it. Give me his name."

Ellie flipped the card over. "Mac Carmichael."

"Oh, damn."

Oh, damn?

"Oh, damn what?"

"Ellie, you're stuck. He is a major pain in the butt, so not even finding him a real full-time maid would fix this. He'd never change a deal he's already made. But he's also somebody Cain's been courting for years."

"Courting?"

"His family owns hotels all over the world. Cain's been trying to get in on the construction end. This might be a test for Cain."

Ellie lowered her forehead to her palm. "Which is prob-ably why my intuition wouldn't let me tell him no."

"I'm guessing," Ava agreed. "Okay, here's what we'll do. It doesn't matter where I work, so I'll forward my calls to the Happy Maids office and handle your phone and walk-ins during the day. Then we'll spend an hour or so together every night doing the day's paperwork."

"You'd do that for me?"

"Of course! This isn't just Happy Maids on the line. It's also Cain's business and I'm Cain's assistant. I have to do whatever needs to be done. Beside, I like you."

Ellie laughed. "Okay."

"Okay? Miss Magic, it will be more than okay. We will make it great. You'll do such a good job for Mac that you'll earn all kinds of brownie points for Liz and Happy Maids, and you might just get Cain the 'in' with Carmichael Incorporated that he's been lobbying for for years."

Ellie sat up. "Yeah. You're right. This is a good thing."

"This is potentially a very good thing," Ava agreed. "And I will do anything at all you need me to do."

"Handling the office during the day should be all the help I need."

"I'll be over in an hour."

"Bring a key because I have to leave right now. Mr. Carmichael wants me at his house in—" she glanced down at the card again "—Coral Gables in an hour, and I need to pack a bag if I'm going to be living there."

"You better get a move on."

"Okay. And Ava?"

"Yes."

Ellie winced. "You might want to stop on your way and buy a tank top and shorts."

Ava laughed. "How about if I just call an HVAC repairman?"

"That'll do it, too. I'll see you tonight."

Mac Carmichael raced his Bentley along the winding streets of Coral Gables and onto his driveway. He stopped at the gate, punched a code into the box on the left, opening the gate, and then roared up the stone drive to the side of his huge house. The garage door opened with another press of a button and he zipped inside. As the door closed behind him, he hopped out of his car, walked through the garage, into the butler's pantry then into the huge gourmet kitchen.

His blond-haired six-year-old daughter, Lacy, sat at the long weathered-wood table by the French doors, coloring. Nine-month-old son Henry sat in a highchair beside her. His former nanny and current next-door neighbor, Mrs. Pomeroy, wiped baby food off his mouth with a wet cloth.

"How did it go?"

He sighed. "Well, I found someone."

"Great."

"I'm not sure. She's—" Tall and blond and so good-looking he damned near turned around and sought out another agency. "Well, she seems a little spacey."

Eighty-year-old Elmira Pomeroy laughed. "Spacey? Is she a drinker?"

"No, she's just—" inappropriately dressed, too pretty for words "—kind of odd."

"Are you sure you want her around your kids?"

"She's not *that* kind of odd. Besides, I don't have a choice. I need total and complete privacy. I can't risk hiring a big impersonal firm or someone who doesn't need me enough to keep her silence."

"You think she's made the connection yet that if she does well her boss's husband could make millions?"

He tossed his suit coat over the back of a chair. "I'm hoping. If she hasn't yet, one call to anybody in Cain's office will get her the info. That should be the carrot on the stick that keeps her here long enough for me to find someone." He leaned in over Lacy. "Hey, baby. What are you doing?"

She gave him a patient look. "Coloring."

"Why don't you put on your swimsuit and we'll take a dip while Mrs. Pomeroy is still here for Henry."

Her heart-shaped face wreathed in smiles. Her blue eyes danced with delight. "Okay!"

She raced from the room and Mac pulled Henry from his highchair. "And how are you today?"

Blond-haired, blue-eyed Henry slapped a chubby fist on his father's cheek.

"Feisty, I see."

"You better believe he's been feisty." Mrs. Pomeroy took his bottle from the warmer and tested the temperature. "I'm not sure if he tired himself out enough that he'll fall asleep immediately after he drinks this or if he's too wound up to sleep at all."

"If you have any problems, come and get me from the pool."

Mrs. Pomeroy's wrinkled face fell in sympathetic lines. "No. You take the time with Lacy. You both could use a few minutes of fun."

"I'm fine. I don't want to shirk my responsibility to the kids."

"You're a good dad."

He pulled in a breath and turned away, trying to make light of her compliment. "I only do what any father should do."

That was why it never would have even crossed his mind to desert his children the way their mother had. He couldn't believe any person would be so narcissistic that she'd abandon her kids just because a second child had been inconvenient to her career. Pamela had been so angry to be pregnant again when she'd read the results of her early pregnancy test that she'd packed a bag, left him and filed for divorce within days. She returned to Hollywood, California, where she immediately resurrected her movie career.

Nine months later, she handed Henry over to Mac. She visited once a month, saying it was difficult to fly across the country anymore than that. But on her last visit she told Mac she might not be able to visit in July. The movie she had made while pregnant with Henry was being released and she would be making the rounds of talk shows promoting it. Mac tried not to panic, but he couldn't help it. If anybody asked Pamela about her divorce or her kids, he had absolutely no idea what she'd say. But he did know that if she mentioned their names, he and the kids would become fodder for the paparazzi.

He'd lived his entire life with bodyguards, alarm systems and armor-plated limos. He'd thought he knew how it felt to live under lock and key, but that was nothing compared to living in a fishbowl. As the ex-husband of a movie star with custody of that movie star's kids, protection and visibility had risen to a whole new level. Not only were his kids targets for kidnappers and extortionists because of his money, but their mother's career could put their faces on the front page of every tabloid in the world. He'd had to go to extreme measures to protect them, and even with those measures in place he wasn't quite sure they were safe.

"You're thinking about that crappy wife of yours again aren't you?"

"No."

Mrs. P. laughed. "Right. You always scowl before a morning of fun with your daughter in the pool." Satisfied with the temperature of the milk in Henry's bottle, she took Henry from Mac's arms. "You know what you need? A good woman to replace the crappy one."

Mac laughed. "It will be a cold frosty day in hell before I trust another woman."

Mrs. P. harrumphed as she headed for the door. "Don't let one bad apple spoil the whole bunch."

Lacy skipped into the room dressed in a bright blue one-piece swimsuit. Mac lifted her into his arms. It was very easy for Mrs. P. to spout quaint sayings, quite another for Mac to heed their advice. Pamela had broken Lacy's heart when she left. Henry would know a mother who only popped in when the spirit moved her. Mac couldn't risk the hearts of his children a second time.

Ellie debated sliding into one of her Happy Maids uniforms. Nothing said hired help better than a bright yellow ruffled apron and a hairnet. But Mac had suggested she wear jeans and she wasn't taking any chances. If she had to endure being a full-time maid, then she intended for Cain to get the recommendation into Carmichael Incorporated. The best way to do that would be to follow Mac's instructions to the letter.

She slowed her car as she wound through the streets of Coral Gables, looking for the address scrawled on the back of the business card. Finally finding the property, she turned onto the driveway only to come face-to-face with an iron gate. She rolled down her car window, pressed a button marked "visitors" on a small stand just within reach of her car and watched as a camera zoomed in on her. She expected a voice to come through the little box, asking for identification. Instead, within seconds, the gate opened.

Good grief. How rich was this guy?

Slowly maneuvering up the wide stone driveway that was a beautiful yellow, not brick-red or brown or even gray, but beautiful butterscotch-yellow, Ellie swiveled her head from side-to-side, taking in the landscaping. Trees stood behind the black iron fence that surrounded the huge front yard, increasing the privacy. Flower gardens filled with red, yellow and orange hibiscus sprang up in no particular order, brightening the green grass with splashes of color. But it was the house that caused her mouth to fall open. Butterscotch-yellow stucco, with rich cocoa-brown trim and columns that rose to the flat roof overhang, and a sparkling glass front door, the house was unlike anything she'd seen before.

She followed the stone driveway around to the side where she found cocoa-brown garage doors and a less auspicious entryway than the front door. She parked her car and got out.

Oppressive heat and humidity buffeted her, making her tank top and jeans feel like a snowmobile suit. The sounds of someone splashing in a pool caught her attention and she walked around back and stopped. Her mouth gaped.

Rows of wide, flat steps made of the same butterscotch-colored stone as in the driveway led from a wall of French doors in the back of the house to an in-ground pool. Shiny butterscotch-colored tiles intermingled with blue and beige tiles, rimming the pool and also creating a walkway that led to a patio of the same stone as the stairs. Behind the patio was a huge gazebo—big enough for a party, not merely a yard decoration—and beyond the grassy backyard was the canal where a bright white yacht was docked.

"Ellie?"

She glanced at the pool again. Mac Carmichael was swimming with a little girl of around six, probably his daughter.

She edged toward them. Trying to sound confident, she said, "Hi."

The little blonde wearing water wings waved shyly.

Mac wiped both hands down his face and headed for the ladder in the shallow water on the far side of the pool. "I'll be right with you."

She wanted to say, "Take your time," or "Don't get out on my account. I'll find my way to the kitchen," but the sight of Mac pulling himself onto the ladder stopped her cold. His dark swimming trunks clung wetly to his firm behind. Water pulled them down, causing them to slip as he climbed the ladder. By the time he got out of the pool his trunks clung precariously to his lean hips. He walked to a beige-and-white-flowered chaise and grabbed a huge towel.

"You got here quickly."

She stared. With the blue skies of Florida as a backdrop, his eyes turned a color closer to topaz. Water ran in rivulets down the black hair on his chest. His still-dripping swimming trunks hung on to his hips for dear life.

"I...um..." She cleared her throat as attraction rumbled through her. It had been so long that she'd been overwhelmingly attracted to a man that she'd missed the symptoms. But here they were. Sweaty palms. Stuttering heart. Inability to form a coherent sentence.

Now she knew why her intuition wouldn't let her allow Mac to leave the Happy Maids office. It wasn't because of Cain. It was because she was attracted to Mac.

Telling herself not to panic, she could handle one little attraction, she smiled. Her intuition might have brought her here for a frivolous reason, but once Ava had told her about Cain wanting an "in" with Mac, she knew she couldn't back out. Liz had saved her when she desperately needed someone. Now she finally had a chance to repay the favor. This was a mission. "I just had to run home to put on jeans and pack a bag."

He motioned to the steps. "You go on up. It's too hot for you to stand out here in this heat in those jeans. As soon as I get Lacy from the pool I'll be in."

This time she could say, "No hurry. I'll be fine," because she seriously needed a minute alone to compose herself. How did one man get so lucky as to not only be rich and live in a house that took her breath away, but also be so good-looking he rivaled the pristine Florida sky?

"Just go up the stairs and turn left, into the kitchen. We'll be there in a minute."

She nodded and started up the steps, feeling as if she were walking the stairs to a museum or some other prestigious building rather than someone's residence. Of course, she wasn't exactly well versed in what a "normal" home should look like. She'd grown up in foster homes until she was seventeen when she ran away. Then she'd slept on the streets and fought tooth and nail just to find something to eat each day until she met Sam. She'd stayed with him, enduring increasing verbal and emotional abuse until the night the abuse became physical. Then she'd run. A Friend Indeed couldn't take her in because they were a charity chartered to care for women with children, but Liz had offered her her couch and ultimately a job. After four years with Happy Maids, interacting with Liz and the friends she'd made through A Friend Indeed, she was only now coming to understand what normal relationships were.

So, she could forgive herself for being a tad awestruck by this house. She might clean for Miami's elite but this guy was in a class by himself, and from the outside, his house absolutely looked like a museum.

Pushing open the second door of the four French doors lining the back wall of the house, she found herself standing between a huge kitchen on the left and a comfy family room on the right. Decorated with an overstuffed brown leather sofa and chairs with shiny cherrywood end tables and a huge flat-screen TV between bookcases that ran along the entire back wall, that part of the open floor plan appeared to be where the family did most of their living.

That she liked.

But only a few steps into the kitchen, she swallowed hard. The stove had eight burners. The refrigerator was actually hidden behind panels of the same cherrywood as the cabinets. Copper pots and pans hung from a rack above the stove. Pale salmon-colored granite countertops accented the rich cabinets. A sink with a tall copper faucet sat in the middle of the center island and another sat in a counter along a far wall. Crystal gleamed behind the glass doors of all the cabinets on the right wall.

She looked around in awe. She'd been in kitchens almost as elaborate as this one. She did, after all, clean for some fairly wealthy people. But men in Mac's caliber weren't wealthy. They were beyond wealthy. They didn't hire weekly cleaning services. They had full-time employees and gourmet kitchens big enough to cook food for parties attended by hundreds of people. As a Happy Maid she only cleaned, didn't cook for any of her clients.

She glanced around again, her mouth slightly open, fear tightening her chest.

She grabbed the cell phone she had stashed in her jeans pocket and hit a speed dial number.

"Ava, I think I'm gonna need a cook book."

CHAPTER TWO

A FEW minutes later, Mac and Lacy entered the kitchen. "Lacy, this is Ellie."

Ellie smiled at the wet-haired little girl wrapped in a bright blue towel. "Nice to meet you."

Lacy glanced down shyly. "Nice to meet you too."

"Ellie's going to be staying with us while we look for a replacement for Mrs. Devlin."

Lacy nodded.

"So why don't you go upstairs and change out of your swimsuit?"

"I could help her," Ellie suggested, eager to do a good job more than to get out of the kitchen. She no longer had a problem being alone with Mac. He was definitely good-looking, and everything female inside of her had absolutely taken notice of his ropey muscles and firm butt in his swim trunks. But being attracted to him was wildly inappropriate. People in his tax bracket didn't mingle with the help. And people in her tax bracket would be foolish to drool or harbor crushes. She'd be safe with him.

Mac shook his head. "Lacy's fine on her own. I'd like to show you to your room and talk about the job a bit while Henry's still napping."

"Henry is your son?"

"Yes." Mac winced. "He's only nine months old. I hope that's not a problem."

Spending a few weeks with a baby a problem? Ellie nearly laughed. She didn't have brothers and sisters. The foster homes she'd lived in only took children, not babies. And after Sam she'd vowed she'd never have another "serious" relationship, which put kids out of reach for her. She'd babysat a time or two for new mothers who lived in A Friend Indeed houses, so she knew how to care for a baby. But she'd never be a mother herself. Having such a lovely block of time with a baby would be pure joy.

"Actually, it's kind of a thrill for me to take care of a baby."

Her words appeared to startle Mac. His face bloomed with happy surprise. His eyes gleamed. His lips bowed upward, into a breathtaking smile. It was so appealing, so genuine, so gorgeous, she was sure it could move mountains. The air thinned in her lungs and for a few seconds she struggled for breath, but she'd already recognized this attraction would come to nothing. He was her employer and she was his employee. That was that. Even if she had to pretend to cough to recoup her air supply every time he smiled at her, he'd never have a clue that he took her breath away.

"Is your bag in the trunk?"

"Yes."

"We'll get that first then I'll show you to your quarters."

"Great." She headed for the door and he followed her. Confused that he was coming with her, she stopped. "I only have one small suitcase. I can get it."

Mac shook his head. "My mother would shoot me for making a lady carry her own bag."

His courtesy caught her off guard. Employers were not supposed to help their employees. Or even be overly nice to them for that matter. And she didn't want him to. She wanted their relationship to be as professional as possible. Decorum was what would keep her safe. She hadn't slept alone in a house with a man since Sam and part of her would be shimmying with fear except this wasn't a personal relationship. It was a professional relationship. And as long as they both abided by that, she'd be fine.

"The bag won't weigh any more than the laundry baskets I'll be carrying down the stairs to the washer."

"Washer and dryer are upstairs." He headed to the left. "Besides, this will be a good opportunity for me to familiarize you with this part of the house."

Relieved that the trip to her car had more of a purpose than just a courtesy—which was inappropriate—she nodded and he led her through the butler's pantry. The cupboards were the same rich cherrywood as the kitchen. The countertops the same salmon-colored granite. When he reached the door at the back, he opened it and motioned for her to precede him.

Stepping into the garage, she took note of the four cars—a Bentley, a Corvette, a black Suburban and a Mercedes—and could have happily swooned. But she knew better. Just as she couldn't even once let her attraction to her new employer show, it was bad form to admire his possessions.

He stepped in front of her again to quickly open the door. Her beat-up compact car came into view. He said nothing—commenting on her possessions would have been bad form for *him*—and waited while she hit the button on her key fob and popped the trunk.

Without a word, he pulled out her suitcase. Because he still wore his swimming trunks she could see the muscles of his arm bunch and his chest ripple with the simple movement. She averted her eyes instead of reacting, firmly putting herself in "household employee" mode where she belonged.

Retracing their steps, she reached the garage entry first and pulled open the door for him.

"Your suitcase weighs about two pounds. I could have gotten the door."

"I know."

Still, she hustled to get ahead of him to open the door to the butler's pantry. She knew her place and she fully intended to stay in it.

Seeing her stilted smile, a shiver of something worked its way through Mac. He'd grown up around servants and knew that technically Ellie should have gotten her own bag. He also knew she felt duty-bound to open the door for him. Yet, when she mentioned going out to her car an odd stirring of unease started in his stomach and worked its way to his chest. He couldn't let her carry her own bag. It felt ungentlemanly.

He chalked it up to their unusual meeting. He hadn't met her as a household employee, but as a woman who was currently running the company he'd needed to cajole into his employ. So he wasn't seeing her as an employee first, but a woman. An equal. Though that wasn't exactly good, he could control that. He could even shift their positions back to employer and employee.

Just as soon as he got her settled.

After all, he had sort of manipulated her into taking a job she hadn't wanted. And he wasn't being forthright even now. When he discovered Pamela's new movie was to be released next month, he'd bought the empty house next to Mrs. Pomeroy and put it in the name of one of his family's smaller corporations so he and his kids could disappear.

Ellie didn't know any of that. She didn't need the information, but more than that her being in the dark was another layer of protection for Mac. As long as she didn't know anything, she couldn't accidently talk to a reporter in disguise as a grocery bagger.

He was keeping her in the dark, forcing her into a job she normally wouldn't have done. A little social nicety wasn't out of line.

In the kitchen, she faced him with a pretty smile. Her full lips turned upward. Her amber eyes sparkled. The blond hair that floated around her head to her shoulders gave her the look of an angel.

"Where to?"

Okay. Maybe this attraction would be a little harder to handle than he'd imagined. She was pretty and sweet. Agreeable. Genuine. She looked like a woman who couldn't tell a lie if her life depended on it, like somebody he could trust with his life. He wanted to melt into a puddle at her feet, to tell her his secrets, ask for her help protecting his kids.

He almost snorted a laugh. Right. With the exception of Mrs. Pomeroy, the last woman he trusted ran out on those same kids. He already knew his instincts about women were way off-kilter. He didn't need another experiment with a woman to prove it.

"Turn right and go up the back stairs."

She frowned. "I don't have quarters near the kitchen?"

"Since you'll be the one waking with Henry in the middle of the night, you need to be close to him."

She hesitated. He couldn't figure out why she'd want to be by the kitchen. She was far too thin to be a midnight snacker. She could want assurance that she wouldn't disturb him when she woke to make Lacy's breakfast—

Or maybe she wanted private space? Damn. He'd forgotten about that. She wasn't normally a live-in employee. She probably didn't know how she'd get downtime.

"When I'm home, I care for the kids. With the exception of getting up with Henry for his 2:00 a.m. feeding when I go back to work. That will be your domain. So you can go to your room any time you're not busy. You can watch TV all you want. You have use of the pool, and you can also leave when I'm here if your work is all caught up."

She nodded, but didn't look reassured. Still, she started up the stairs.

Averting his eyes to resist the temptation of watching her bottom as she walked the thin flight of steps, Mac said, "First door on the right is yours."

She tossed a shaky smile over her shoulder. "So I'm right by the stairway?"

He almost laughed. It sounded as if she wanted assurance that she could make a quick getaway. "Yes. You're right by the stairway."

She breathed a sigh of relief and his brow furrowed. Maybe he hadn't been so far off the mark about the quick getaway? Or at least the possibility of one. She wasn't normally a live-in worker. If assurance that she had an escape route pleased her, then who was he to argue?

In the upstairs hall, she turned right and entered the suite. But she stopped so quickly Mac almost ran into her back.

Hesitantly stepping into the room, she smoothed her hand along the arm of a simple yellow sofa that sat beside a matching chair and in front of a wide-screen TV. Her head turned from side to side as she walked to the door that led to the bedroom. Then she gasped.

"This is gorgeous."

He ambled up beside her and glanced into the room which, he supposed, was pretty with its black four-poster bed and pale gold spread and matching curtains.

"It's a bit of a perk since our maid also has to be a nanny."

This time when she faced him her angelic smile had been replaced by one of sheer joy. Her amber eyes were so brilliant they virtually shone.

"Maybe I should take this job permanently," she said with a laugh.

Bowled over by the power in her smile, he nearly said, "That's a great idea." Luckily he stopped himself. First, he was too darned attracted to her to keep her forever. Second, she was a stranger hinting for a full-time position caring for his kids. He knew all the employees of Happy Maids were bonded, which meant they'd passed routine background checks, but he'd still ordered his security team to do a full background check on Ellie after she'd agreed to take the job. Within twenty minutes Mac knew she'd never been in jail, never been arrested, never even had an unpaid parking ticket. Which meant his children were somewhat safe with her.

But he still didn't feel he knew enough to be comfortable leaving her alone with his kids. Lacy and Henry were everything to him. He wouldn't trust them with just anybody. He'd ordered his security team to keep looking into her past. By this time tomorrow, he hoped to know everything there was to know about Ellie Swanson. If he found anything at all in the report he didn't like he might actually be asking her to leave, not inviting her to stay permanently.

He walked over to the door leading to the nursery. "Henry's in here."

She followed him into the huge room decorated with rainbows and unicorns, white rockers and fuzzy lime-green throw rugs. Henry stirred. Mac leaned in to check on him and Ellie leaned in, too.

She whispered, "Oh, we're going to wake him?"

Her breath fanned across his cheek. The scent of her cologne wafted to him. Her upper arm brushed against his. He swallowed and decided he'd better speed up his search for a permanent maid. He'd never been more aware of a woman. Let alone someone who was technically help.

But he hadn't met her as help and she didn't behave like help. And if he didn't soon establish a boss/housekeeper relationship between them, this attraction could be trouble. He could embarrass her, or worse, embarrass himself. Then her entire stay would be awkward.

Henry woke and let out a little cry to awaken his voice before he shrieked in earnest. Mac hoisted the baby into his arms before he terrified his new nanny.

To his surprise, though, she laughed. "Oh, gosh, he's cute." She tweaked his cheek. "And listen to those lungs! You're going to be a rock star someday, aren't you, little pumpkin!"

Henry stopped crying and peered at her curiously.

It appeared Mac wasn't the only Carmichael male who was being thrown off-kilter by this woman's looks and far too casual behavior.

"Henry, this is Ellie. She's going to be caring for you when Daddy can't. Ellie, this is Henry."

"Can I hold him?"

"Sure."

She took the baby from his arms with the ease of someone accustomed to holding a baby.

"Hey, sweetie," she said, bouncing him a bit. But Henry only continued to stare.

I'm right with you, kid. She's so beautiful I could stare at her all day too, Mac thought, taking a step back out of range of her cologne. He walked to the changing table and retrieved a diaper and other necessary items to clean up the baby before putting him into a new outfit. "Bring him here. I'm sure he needs to be changed."

Ellie smiled at him. "I can handle this. You go and do whatever you would usually be doing right now."

"No."

"No?" She took a few steps closer to the changing table. "I thought I was here to care for your kids?"

"Yes, you are. But," he said, keeping his gaze and attention on Henry as he removed his diaper, "as I've already mentioned, I'll care for the children while I'm here."

"Okay."

She didn't sound at all understanding of his position that he'd be caring for his own kids. But Mac didn't feel the need to explain that he had to make up for his ex-wife's neglect by being available to his kids as much as he could be. Through his peripheral vision he saw that she stood off to the side, watching him, making Mac nervous until he realized she was waiting for instructions.

Mac glanced up at her. "Why don't you go to your room and unpack your bag? When I'm done with Henry, I'll give you the rest of the tour of the house."

Ten minutes later, Mac knocked on her bedroom door and stepped inside, a clean and happy Henry on his arm.

Closing the closet door where she'd stowed her suitcase, Ellie faced him. "Ready for the tour?"

"Yes." Mac led her out of her suite and to the right. He pointed at the door beside the nursery door. "This leads to my suite."

"Okay."

She didn't like the warmth that bubbled in her middle with the realization that their bedrooms were so close. Fear or apprehension wouldn't have surprised her. But anticipation? That was ridiculous and wrong. She'd sworn off men forever. The proximity of their bedrooms shouldn't matter. Plus, her suite had its own bathroom. She wouldn't be venturing into the hall in her nightclothes or wrapped in a towel before or after a shower—neither would he. She had nothing to fear and nothing to worry about—except maybe this crazy attraction which seemed to have a life of its own.

Mac opened the next door. With a motion of his hand he invited her to peek into the pink-and-white room. "And this is Lacy's room. Also close enough for you to hear her if something happens."

Glad to have her mind moving off his master suite and to the kids, Ellie said, "Good."

Walking again, they passed eye-popping red statues and etchings done in cocoa-brown ink. Behind a curving cherrywood staircase, a wall of windows displayed a panoramic view of the canal. Sharp, contemporary accent chairs with chrome arms and legs and nubby yellow fabric backs and seats sat by tall, thin chrome lamps. The floor was a warm honey-colored hardwood. Once again she thought of a museum.

"These two doors," Mac said, pointing to the right and then the left, "lead to two guest suites."

They turned a corner. Mac pointed at two doors on opposite sides of the hall. "Two more guest suites."

"Of course."

"I don't have guests often," Mac continued, leading her down the hall. Over his shoulder, blue-eyed Henry grinned toothlessly at Ellie.

She smiled and waved.

"And won't be having any guests at all until I've hired a permanent maid." He paused at a set of double doors. After shifting Henry on his forearm, he opened them, revealing a laundry room complete with a bright red washer and dryer, a folding table, carts, baskets and cherrywood cabinets that she assumed held laundry detergent and the like.

Smiling her professional household employee smile, Ellie said, "Okay."

"You can easily gather everyone's laundry, wash it, dry it, press it in here and return it to the proper room."

With that he closed the doors and directed her back down another hall.

"As you can see, we're making a full circle. These steps," Mac said as they approached the set of back stairs, "are the same ones we used to get up here."

They started down the wooden steps and at the bottom turned left to enter the kitchen.

"We have a very simple floor plan."

Glancing around the kitchen, Ellie said, "Yes."

"Okay, now for the first floor."

Mac led her out of the kitchen, down a short hall and turned right into a room that had to be the playroom. The back wall held cherrywood bookcases and built-in cupboards, probably for storing toys, and a wide-screen TV. A thick brown-and-red print rug sat in the middle of the hardwood floor. Otherwise, the room was without furniture. Unless you counted the bright blue plastic table and chairs with accompanying yellow plastic dishes and cups where Lacy sat—probably having an imaginary tea party—and the beige plastic stove, refrigerator and sink that Ellie recognized from her last trip to a toy store.

Looking up from her tea party, Lacy said, "Hi, Daddy."

"Hi, sweetie. You remember Ellie."

She nodded enthusiastically, her fine blond hair bobbed around her.

"Hi, Lacy. I like your playroom."

Lacy only grinned and nodded again.

Mac walked over to his daughter, who tugged on his pant leg to get his attention.

"Daddy, I'm hungry."

Though Lacy tried to whisper, her voice came out loud and clear.

"Okay." Mac faced Ellie. "Can we finish our tour later?"

She nodded. "Sure."

Mac said, "Great," and headed for the doorway on the right. "Let's go make something for lunch."

Lacy's face brightened as Ellie's stomach fell to the floor. She hadn't had time to get the cookbook yet! What would she do if Mac asked for something Ellie had no idea how to prepare?

Before she could panic Lacy said, "Can we have peanut butter sandwiches and ice cream?"

Walking into the hall, Mac laughed. "We'll negotiate the ice cream after you've eaten the sandwich."

Still carrying Henry, Mac left the room with happy Lacy skipping behind him. Ellie took a minute to breathe a sigh of relief before she bounded out of the room. She caught up with them in the kitchen.

Sliding Henry into a highchair, Mac said, "Now that I think about it, Ellie, you could actually finish the tour of the rest of the house by yourself. Dining room and living room are at the front of the house. Over there is the family room." He pointed at the area beside the kitchen with the leather furniture and big-screen TV. "My office is above the garage, but there's no reason for you to go there."

He straightened away from the highchair. "While I feed the kids, you can make a list of what needs to be done cleaningwise. Then when the children and I are done, you can clean the kitchen and get started with supper."

"Okay."

He smiled patiently. "Okay."

Not exactly sure what happened with lunch and feeling oddly dismissed, Ellie turned and walked out of the kitchen. It wasn't that she had a burning need to make peanut butter sandwiches. She felt unnecessary. He'd insisted that she start today, yet she wasn't doing any of the things he'd hired her to do. No. He wouldn't *let* her do any of the things he'd hired her to do.

Her intuition tried to tell her that something was wrong with this situation, but she ignored it, as she intended to do for the rest of her stay here. After all, her intuition had already steered her wrong about taking this job. She wasn't letting it in on any more decision making.

And she certainly wasn't about to let it spark her imagination. That would only result in her becoming too curious about this man and his adorable children and asking some very inappropriate questions. Like what kind of woman would leave such wonderful kids and such a handsome, courteous husband?

Unless Mac had only been putting on a good front for her?

Because he had custody of his kids she automatically assumed he was a good man.

But what if he wasn't?

What if he had his kids because he was an overbearing rich guy who threw his weight around to get everything he wanted?

What if she was about to spend the next several weeks living with another man like Sam?

CHAPTER THREE

AFTER lunch, Mac took the kids out on his yacht for the afternoon. Standing in the kitchen in front of the French doors, Ellie watched the boat pull away from the dock, grateful for a few minutes to herself.

She had silenced her concerns that Mac might be like Sam by reminding herself of two things. First, she didn't know Mac. She shouldn't jump to conclusions. And second, Mac genuinely seemed to like his kids, to like spending time with them. So what if he'd nudged her out of lunch and really wasn't letting her be the nanny? He might have done it unconsciously. She had no idea how long he'd been without a maid and nanny. But it could have been long enough that caring for his kids was now second nature. And if Ellie didn't soon stop acting like a high-strung spinster, suspicious of every man she met, she'd lose this job, and Cain and Liz would be the ones to suffer.

Her cell phone rang. She looked down and saw Ava's number in caller ID.

"Hey."

"Hey! I'm at the gate. Now what?"

Ellie glanced around. Not only did she not know how to open the gate, but Mac wasn't here to show her. She couldn't even attempt to please this privileged family on her limited knowledge of cooking. She had to get that cookbook. "I don't know. I don't know how to open the gate and I can't ask Mac because he just took the kids out on his boat."

"Well, all I have is the cookbook. Why don't you come to me and I'll pass it through the gate to you?"

Ellie sighed with relief. "Good idea."

Feeling like a criminal, she snuck out the front door of the echoing mansion, raced down the front yard and reached through the gate bars to get the cookbook from Ava.

"Thanks."

Cain Nestor's fifty-five-year-old assistant peered over her black frame glasses at Ellie. "Tell me I'll be able to get through the gate tonight when we have to debrief about Happy Maids."

"You will. I swear," Ellie said, walking backward up the grassy front yard to return to the house.

"Good. I'll see you tonight," Ava called, but Ellie was already running toward the door. Cookbook under her arm, she tiptoed up the silent hall to the kitchen even though she knew she was alone in the house. Mac had said he and his children would be gone the entire afternoon, yet she still felt as if she was doing something wrong.

But she wasn't. *She could cook.* She simply hadn't memorized recipes for anything beyond burgers and spaghetti. All she had to do was find a recipe, prepare the food, and serve it like a good maid, then Cain and Liz would both get the recommendations they needed.

Sitting at the weathered table by the French doors, she took the cookbook out of the plastic bookstore bag. *Easy Main Dishes in Under An Hour.* Ellie laughed. Ava was nothing if not perceptive! This should be a cinch.

She perused the recipes, with one eye on the canal so she would see the Carmichael family if they returned unexpectedly. Spotting a recipe she liked—penne pasta with portabella mushrooms and red and yellow peppers— she took the book with her as she walked around the kitchen, checking for supplies.

The well-stocked refrigerator had both red and yellow peppers and portabella mushrooms. The cabinet held penne pasta. Next she found the ingredients for the Alfredo sauce. Interestingly, in the last cabinet on the row closest to the door leading to the stairway, she also found the controls for the gate, including a small computer monitor that displayed the feed from the video camera. One button said "Open gate." One said "Close gate." A system couldn't get any simpler than that.

Because the meal would only take an hour to prepare, she decided to do laundry and some light cleaning while Mac and the kids were out on the ocean.

She found baskets of dirty clothes in each of the kids' bathrooms, but she stopped at the master suite. Mac hadn't even opened the door to let her peek in as he'd done with Lacy's room. A bedroom was such a private space, it felt like an invasion to even look inside. Forget about walking in. She'd feel like an interloper. She'd already had to talk herself out of being suspicious of this guy. She didn't want to give her free-wheeling imagination any more grist for the mill!

Maybe tomorrow she'd be adjusted enough to collect his laundry, but she'd handled enough for today.

After sorting the kids' clothes, she put a load into the washer then returned downstairs, this time using the fancy curved cherrywood stairway.

She walked past the living room with shiny marble floor, heavy tapestry drapes and ultra-modern furniture with glass tables. Not exactly her taste, but in keeping with the rest of the museum-like décor. The room wasn't even in need of a light dusting. So she checked the dining room, playroom, sitting room and den and found them all in the same spotless condition. She walked to the kitchen where she grabbed the notepad on which she'd made the list of everything that needed to be done as Mac had suggested, and began arranging things in the best order for cleaning. Whether the rooms "needed" dusting or not, she would begin a rotation that maintained the spotless condition of this home.

By the time the yacht returned, she had a schedule developed that would assure the entire house would be kept spotless, the laundry would be done and three meals would be prepared.

Chopping the peppers, she watched out the window as Mac carried Henry on his arm and led his daughter up the dock to the backyard and toward the house. She fought the suspicion again that something was wrong with this picture because she didn't know what it was. It wasn't something she could see or something she'd heard, only a sense she had. If she just had something substantial to base the feeling on, she'd know how to handle it. Instead, she had only an unhappy imagination that was making her crazy.

Annoyed with herself for not dropping this, she waited for them to enter the kitchen, but after fifteen minutes she realized they had probably come in through another door. Two seconds later, Mac walked into the kitchen wearing jeans and a T-shirt.

"Everything okay?"

Trying to behave like a normal maid, not an overly suspicious idiot, she smiled shakily at him. "Great. I spent the afternoon creating a cleaning schedule, so I can hit the ground running tomorrow."

"There's no rush." Mac opened the refrigerator and snagged an apple. "The place is immaculate. It can go a day or two without being dusted. I want you to get accustomed to the house and the cleaning end of things these next few days so that when I go back to work, the kids can be your priority." He caught her gaze. "I also want this time for the kids to get accustomed to seeing you around the house. To get to know you before you're their primary caregiver."

Okay. See? He had a good explanation for having her around the kids, but not actually interacting with them. He was giving her time to get accustomed to the house and giving the kids time to get accustomed to her. That made more sense than to think something was wrong with him.

"I'll be fine with the kids." That she could say with complete confidence. "Helping some friends—" She almost said the women living in A Friend Indeed houses, but thought the better of it. She didn't really know Mac and most of the charity's work was confidential to protect the identities of the women seeking shelter. "I've babysat, played board games and gone to the beach more times than I can count."

He crunched a bite of the apple, chewed then swallowed and said, "Great." He paused for a second before he added, "This job won't last long. My assistant is working with two employment agencies now, looking for a replacement for Mrs. Devlin. She'll do initial interviews. I'll do the second interview."

"So you should have a replacement in three weeks?" Ellie asked hopefully.

He winced. "More like four."

Liz's entire honeymoon.

"I'm sorry that I sort of strong-armed you into this. But my kids are important to me and I don't want just anybody around them."

Surprised, but pleased that he'd apologized—once again confirming that he was a nice guy and she had to stop looking for bad things about him—she nodded. "I get that. We'll be fine."

"And there's one other thing I forgot to mention. I'd prefer that you not tell anyone where you're working."

She winced. "I'm sorry but I already told Ava. She's helping me with Happy Maids. But you don't have to worry," she hastily added, not wanting to anger him unnecessarily. "Ava works for Cain. He owns five businesses. She knows how to be discreet."

"Okay." He turned to leave the room, but suddenly faced her again. "What are you making for dinner?"

"Penne pasta with red and yellow peppers." She glanced up at him. "I never asked what time you'd like to eat."

"I eat with Lacy, which means we always eat before six."

"Okay." That gave her forty minutes. "I better get a move on then."

Henry's soft cries poured from the baby monitor and Ellie froze. Already her impulse was to drop everything and rush to get the baby when he cried. But she waited to see what Mac wanted her to do.

He said, "I'll get him," and headed for the back stairway. "As I said, when I'm here, I take care of the kids."

This time his doing her job didn't bother her. He'd explained that he wanted her to get accustomed to things… the house, the cleaning schedule… All that was good. It even made more sense from the perspective of his wanting to give the kids a chance to get accustomed to her.

She had nothing to worry about.

She gathered the items from the recipe and began preparing the sauce. Her eyes on the list of ingredients, she measured and poured milk, cheese and butter into the pan. Stirring the sauce as it heated, she tried to keep her mind on her cooking, but couldn't.

The instincts she kept trying to ignore tiptoed into her conscious, whispering that Mac wasn't being nice. He was keeping his kids away from her because he didn't really trust her. Sure, he'd apologized about strong-arming her, and, yes, he had a good explanation about why he was doing her job…but there was something in the air in this house. Something that didn't quite fit.

Something…

The sauce in the pot bubbled over and Ellie jumped back out of the way with a squeak as she snapped off the gas burner.

She heard the sound of Mac racing down the stairs and quickly placed her body in front of the stove to hide the mess.

"Everything okay?" he asked, walking into the kitchen with Henry on his arm.

"Great."

"I thought I heard a squeal."

The odd feeling returned again. He had every right to investigate a squeal, but the tone of his voice just didn't sit right.

Of course, she might be overanalyzing because she was nervous about having just burned a big part of his dinner!

"I… Um…" She swallowed to gather her courage. "My sauce just boiled over."

"Oh. Okay, if everything's under control the kids and I are going to take a short walk."

He took it so casually that Ellie blinked in surprise as Mac turned away. Sam would have screamed at her for hours for ruining dinner, proving Mac wasn't a full-fledged grouch or even really a control freak. So what the heck was going on here?

As Mac called, "Lacy!" Ellie noticed Henry had on a straw hat and a lightweight one-piece pajama that covered his entire body to protect him from the sun. Ellie didn't criticize Mac's diligence. But it did further the theory that he was very protective of his children and she'd better do the absolute best job she could do when she was alone with them—

Ah! Now she got it.

The parents of the kids she typically babysat for trusted her. This guy didn't know her. So how could he trust her? He couldn't! That was why he seemed to be keeping the kids from her. Until he got to know her he'd probably huddle over Henry and Lacy rather than let her alone with them…and probably also question her every move. His distrust could even be the "odd" thing she sensed in the air of this house.

Lacy ran into the room. She also wore a straw hat to protect her from the sun. "I'm ready, Daddy."

Mac said, "Let's go." Then he and the kids trooped out of the kitchen.

Ellie spun around and looked at the milk-covered burner on the stove with a groan. She grabbed her cell phone from her jeans pocket.

"Ava, can you get a jar of store-bought Alfredo sauce here in twenty minutes?"

Ava laughed. "Ellie, you're going to wear me out."

"This time I can let you in the gate."

"Great. I'll fill you in on the Happy Maids stuff while I'm there."

Twenty minutes later, Ava arrived with two jars of Alfredo sauce and the maids' time sheets to be signed for payroll. As Ellie poured the penne pasta, portabella mush-rooms and red and yellow peppers into a casserole dish and then covered them with Alfredo sauce and popped them into the oven, Ava briefed her on Happy Maids' day.

"Nothing out of the ordinary happened. The houses were cleaned as scheduled. The Maids have their jobs for tomorrow."

"Thanks, Ava."

"You're welcome. Now, I have to get home. I'll see you tomorrow afternoon around this time." Ava headed for the butler's pantry, but stopped and grinned at Ellie. "Don't hesitate to call me if you need something."

Ellie shook her head in dismay. "I'm sorry but this guy is a serious control freak." She'd finally decided to label him a control freak, if only because distrust was such an ugly word and she didn't want Ava to realize she was uncom-fortable. She might want Ellie to leave and she couldn't. Cain and Liz needed for her to do a good job. "I didn't dare risk a mistake."

Ava laughed. "I was teasing. I don't mind you calling me for help. You're doing this as much for my boss as for yours. So we're in this together."

With that Ellie scooted out through the butler's pantry and garage, leaving Ellie to prepare a salad in the twenty minutes it would take to heat the pasta and sauce.

She was just pulling dinner from the oven when Mac and the kids returned.

She greeted them with a smile. "You're right on time."

"Great. We're starving." He ambled to the door. "You may serve us in the formal dining room."

Ellie smiled, breathing a silent sigh of relief that he'd told her what to do and quickly set the table. As she did that, Mac grabbed a jar of baby food, a baby dish and a tiny spoon.

She served the food while Mac fed Henry.

"That'll be all, Ellie."

Ellie nodded in acknowledgement and scurried back into the kitchen. But she opened the swinging door a crack and peeked into the dining room. Watching the happy little family, she amended her opinion of Mac once again. It seemed wrong to call him a control freak when he was looking out for his kids. In some circles that would make him a good dad.

Still, there was the matter of the missing wife. She couldn't reconcile herself to thinking that any woman would give full custody of two adorable children to her husband. Had there been a custody battle? Were these two kids scarred for life?

Of course, his wife could be—Ellie swallowed—dead. Oh, dear. That would certainly raise a whole different set of issues! Including the curiosity of why he hadn't told Ellie, if only to explain whether or not the kids were still dealing with that.

No. He would have told her if his wife were dead. As diligent as he was, he'd want her to be prepared about everything to do with his kids. His wife had to have left.

But where was she? And why had *she* gone, leaving her kids behind?

Telling herself it was none of her business and that she could handle not knowing for one month if it meant that Liz got the recommendations she needed and Cain got the contracts he wanted, Liz began scrubbing pots and wiping the kitchen counters.

When the Carmichaels were finished eating, Mac leaned into the kitchen. "We're done. Lacy and I will be upstairs getting Henry ready for bed."

"Okay."

"Once you've cleaned up, you're done for the day. You may do whatever you wish. It's still hot out, so you might want to take a dip in the pool. The kids and I are in for the night, so it's all yours if you wish. Good night, Ellie."

He pulled out of the room without waiting for her reply and Ellie leaned against the counter with a sigh of relief.

Day one down!

After clearing the dining room and popping the dishes into the dishwasher, Ellie went to her room.

She wouldn't mind a swim, but she hadn't brought a suit. Plus, she needed to get up early the next morning. She set her alarm for four, so that she'd be ready for Lacy whatever time she awoke, then did a quick pirouette in the massive bedroom she'd be staying in for the next month. Her boss's life might be a bit of a mystery. She might wonder what happened to the kids' mom. And she absolutely *had* to get better at cooking. But spending a month in this suite could almost make up for that. It was the lap of luxury.

Running her hand up one of the black posts of the four-poster bed, she noticed the gold decorative rings at the top and sighed dreamily. What must it be like to have so much money that you could have *everything* you wanted, exactly as you wanted it?

Lifting her makeup bag from the black mirrored dresser, she turned and walked into the bathroom. Again, she stopped and stared in awe. Brown travertine tiles on the floor matched the brown tiles in the shower and surrounding the spa tub. This bathroom was as big as the kitchen in her and her roommate Mitzi's apartment.

She set the makeup case on the counter of the double sink with black-and-gold granite countertops, then stripped to make good use of the spa tub. After a nice long soak, she stepped into lightweight pajamas, applied face cream and crawled into bed with a book. Cool silk sheets greeted her and she groaned. There was a definite difference between cleaning someone's house once a week and staying in that house—even if it was as hired help. She certainly hoped she didn't get used to this!

She read until about ten, then turned out the light of the brushed gold lamp on the bedside table and immediately fell asleep.

What seemed like only minutes later Henry's loud crying woke her. Slightly disoriented, she bolted up in bed, wondering what the sound was. But the second burst of crying brought her to full alertness and got her to her feet.

"Henry!" she cried, not even sure if the little boy could hear her. "I'm coming, sweetie!"

Intending to change his diaper and take him downstairs while she warmed a bottle, she ran into the room. As her door opened on the left side of the nursery, Mac's door on the right side of the nursery also opened. Both flew into the room and stopped dead in their tracks.

Her pajamas, though lightweight, were covering. *His* chest was bare above low-riding bottoms. His dark hair was mussed. His eyelids drooped sexily and his brilliant blue eyes were glazed over. He had the sleepy look of a man who cuddled after sex.

The very fact that that popped into her mind shocked her. She couldn't speak. She couldn't move. She'd seen him in swimming trunks that afternoon, but with her brain jumping to inappropriate places and both of them soft and warm from sleep, everything about the moment felt different.

His gaze fell from her pajama top to her bare feet. As it leisurely crawled back up her body again, the haze in his eyes disappeared. She stifled a shiver. The way he had looked at her stole her breath. Not awake enough to monitor his reaction, he'd taken inventory from the top of her head to the tips of her toes and back up again, very obviously liking what he saw.

Their gazes caught and the light in his eyes intensified, sharpened.

Ellie swallowed, told herself to speak and speak now, but nothing came out.

Then Henry screamed.

"I'm sorry, buddy," Mac said, breaking eye contact to race to the crib. He hoisted the little boy into his arms. It fleetingly occurred to Ellie that he was adorable with his son, especially when the baby so eagerly wrapped his chubby arms around his dad's neck, but the ripple of the muscles of his biceps and back as he cuddled Henry caused her heart to stutter in her chest and warmth to pool in her middle.

She took a step back. This attraction was ridiculous. As her boss, he was off-limits for too many reasons to count. But even if he was interested in her, she didn't want to be attracted to him! He was her boss. Cain and Liz needed for her to do a good job. And by God, she would.

She walked over to the crib. "I'll go downstairs and get the bottle."

He peeked over at her. Gooseflesh sprinkled over her entire body. She tried to remind herself that Cain and Liz were depending on her, and that meant she had to behave in a professional manner, but her gaze stayed locked with Mac's.

What was wrong with her? Her intuition was scrambling. Her hormones had executed a coup. And her brain seemed to have gone on vacation.

Finally Mac said, "I'll get it."

Ellie took a breath. "No. That's okay. You change him. I'll get the bottle." She had to get out of this room! "By the time I return, you'll be ready for it so you can feed him."

He nodded, and she walked toward the nursery door, but at the last second she changed her mind and headed for the door of her suite. She closed it behind her then walked through her sitting room to get to the hall. It wasn't that she didn't want him seeing her things. She hadn't scattered her things about. She was a tidy person. It was more that there was something about both of them sleeping so close, with only a nursery to separate them. Something intimate was happening between them and she didn't want him thinking about her any more than she wanted to be thinking about him.

But she would.

Damn it. She knew she would.

What was it about this guy that drew her? Sure, he had beautiful blue eyes. Yes, he was perfect physically with his well-defined muscles that rippled when he moved, and shiny black hair that looked silky smooth and made her itch to run her fingers through it.

But he was...unattainable!

And she didn't know him. Rich people always had secrets in their closets and this guy's very demeanor screamed trouble.

Plus, she didn't want a relationship. Damn it. One day in his company and she'd almost forgotten every lesson she'd learned with Sam!

At the refrigerator, she put her attention on preparing Henry's bottle. Her mind back where it belonged, she got one of the pre-poured bottles of milk from the refrigerator. She heated it to room temperature as she'd been taught by several of the mothers at A Friend Indeed and returned to Henry's room.

Mac sat on the rocking chair with Henry on his lap, his towhead nestled against his daddy's chest. Ellie's heart squeezed.

Fuzzy feminine feelings rose up in her and she suddenly understood why Mac was so appealing to her. No matter what his secrets, he truly loved his kids and somehow or another that hit her right in the maternal instincts. She'd always wanted children and if she'd met someone normal before she'd met Sam her life probably would have been very different.

"Here," she whispered, handing Mac the bottle.

He glanced up at her. Their gazes caught for only a second, but it was long enough for Ellie to feel the sizzle again, reminding her that this attraction wasn't one-side. And *that* was the problem.

"Thanks."

She took a step back. "You're welcome."

Then she turned and all but ran back to her suite.

Even if an employer felt an attraction for the help, most wouldn't let it show. Mac hadn't let it show all day. But being half-asleep, his guard had been down. Nine chances out of ten, he wouldn't even acknowledge this in the morning.

But what if he did?

What if he liked her?

What if living with him for a month was enough that their barriers broke down?

He already had her stuttering and staring. If he made a pass at her, could she resist him?

And what if she didn't?

No one knew better than Ellie that there were consequences to relationships.

Especially relationships with bosses.

CHAPTER FOUR

ELLIE awakened at four, dressed in a clean pair of jeans and yawned her way to the kitchen. To her amazement six-year-old Lacy was waiting for her.

"Lacy?"

From her position on one of the chairs at the table, she peeked at Ellie. "Sorry."

"Oh, that's okay, honey," Ellie said, walking over to the table where the little girl sat. She stooped down to make herself eye-level. "I'm just a little concerned about you being up by yourself."

Lacy leaned her elbow on the table and angled her chin on her fist. She wore pale blue pajamas covered in tiny pink hearts. The color brought out the blue in her eyes and made her wispy pale hair seem even more golden. "I just sit here until somebody gets up."

"Really?"

"Yes. She does. She's fine."

Ellie spun around to face the door when Mac spoke. He stood on the threshold, not in last night's pajama bottoms, but in a pair of sweatpants and a baggy T-shirt. Barefoot, he ambled into the kitchen.

"She likes an egg for breakfast, toast and some blue-berries."

"And a glass of milk," Lacy added with a grin.

Staring at Mac, Ellie told her heart to settle down and her hormones to please take a vacation, but neither listened. Her heart tumbled in her chest and adrenaline surged through her blood. The man was just too good-looking. And he was dedicated to his kids. She'd never met a man who changed diapers and awakened at four without complaint. Yet she still felt something was off.

Suddenly the entire situation began to make sense. He was a great dad, seemingly a good person, and he was gorgeous...so she was attracted to him. But her experience with men wasn't good. So while her hormones were loping off the charts, her common sense was trying to find things wrong with him.

He wasn't a mystery. She was the one with the problem. Or maybe their attraction was the problem.

Still, she was the help and nothing more. From the nonchalant way he drifted into the kitchen and ambled to the table where Lacy sat, Ellie knew he had absolutely no interest in following up on the attraction he felt to her. After all, it was only physical. They hadn't spoken beyond the work required for this job. What they felt for each other couldn't be anything other than a healthy case of sexual attraction.

A good relationship required so much more. Shared interests. Mutual likes and dislikes. Even a shared background would be nice. Her background was so different from his that they probably didn't even share one similar childhood memory! She didn't even need to remember all the other reasons they were wrong for each other. With pasts as different as theirs, none of that mattered.

Reminded of her place, Ellie said, "We're fine here, Mr. Carmichael. You can go back to bed."

Mac gave her a puzzled frown. "Mr. Carmichael?"

Ellie winced. "You never did tell me what to call you."

"I'm Mac." He paused significantly. "*Everyone* calls me Mac."

"Okay, Mac," she said, trying out the name and finding it was much easier to call him by his first name than it should be given that she was his maid. "I'll take care of Lacy's breakfast. You can go on back to bed."

"I'm home. I take care of the kids when I'm home. Remember?"

"Yes, but it's so early."

"So why don't *you* go back to bed?"

She pressed her had to her chest. "Me?"

"There's no point in both of us being up at four."

He wasn't angry and what he said made sense. Now that she'd totally squelched her instincts, the entire situation made perfect sense. She took a step backward, toward the door. "Okay, then. I guess I will go back to bed."

She turned to leave the kitchen, but Mac stopped her. "Ellie?"

She faced him. "Yes?"

"I don't always get up with her. When I'm working I usually sleep through her early-morning-wake-up days. So I appreciate that you're okay with this."

She couldn't believe she'd let her intuition talk her into thinking there was something wrong here. Yes, she might not know where the kids' mom was, but Mac was a normal man. A good dad. A good guy. She had been wrong to be suspicious of him.

She smiled her best professional, I'm-your-maid smile. "You're welcome."

She left the room, glad that everything was handled amicably. But halfway up the stairs she stopped as another question confronted her. Why would a six-year-old get up at four o'clock—or close—every day?

She squeezed her eyes shut. Mac might be an okay guy, but she couldn't dismiss her suspicions so easily. No matter how or why Lacy's mom had left, losing her mom had affected her. Without knowing the truth, Ellie could make a million mistakes with that little girl.

Three hours later, with Lacy fed and back to bed for a morning nap, Mac headed for his office, then realized he couldn't go there because it was too far away. He changed directions and headed for the master suite. Halfway down the hall, his cell phone rang. He glanced at caller ID and saw it was his investigator, and not a moment too soon.

"Hey, Phil."

"Hey, Mac. I've got some news on your new girl."

Mac opened the door to his suite, stepped inside and closed the door behind himself. "Spill."

"Well, she's from Wisconsin."

Walking to one of the two white chairs in front of the never used fireplace, Mac laughed. "You say that as if it's bad, but this is Florida. Lots of us are Northern transplants."

"It's not the part about coming from up north that's bad. Your new housekeeper was a foster child."

That stopped him. "Oh. Why is that bad?"

"It isn't. I mean, it doesn't positively indicate bad things. Lots of foster kids grow up to be perfectly normal. But that's not the end of the story on your temporary maid. She ran away at age seventeen. Didn't finish high school."

"How does a seventeen-year-old support herself in a strange city without an education?"

"That's just it. The possibilities that come to mind aren't good ones. If she worked on the street or under the table, from here on out it's going to be harder and harder to find information."

"I don't care. Whatever it costs, you fill in the blanks of her past."

"Not only is that going to be expensive, but also it will take days."

"Again, I don't care. This woman is going to be caring for my kids. I want to know everything about her."

Phil said, "Will do, boss."

Blowing his breath out on a sigh, Mac disconnected the call and leaned back in his chair. Being attracted to an employee was bad enough; being attracted to someone he didn't know—at all—who had missing pieces of her past was downright foolhardy.

In fact, he'd have to watch her very, very carefully over the next few days as his security team continued their investigation. If she made one move he didn't like, he'd have to let her go. He wasn't worried about the silver or the artwork or even money she might find. He was concerned for his kids. God only knew what Ellie had done in the years after she ran away from home. Without a high school education, as a runaway on the streets, she could have been a thief...or worse.

After doing some cleaning, Ellie once again took out her cookbook and cruised the well-stocked Carmichael cupboards. She found the ingredients for many of the recipes, but she also found boxes of ready-to-cook hamburger dishes, noodle entrées and macaroni and cheese. Maybe the Carmichael pallet wasn't so sophisticated after all? Mac did have a six-year-old, and children did like to eat food they saw on TV. So maybe the thing to do would be prepare simple lunches of the prepackaged foods and cook more elaborate—more nutritious—suppers?

Satisfied with that decision, she headed to her room for a half-hour break before she had to return to the kitchen and prepare lunch. After turning on the television to listen to the day's news, she began taking inventory of the clothes she'd brought. Knowing she'd be here at least a month, she realized the few jeans, shorts and tops she'd packed wouldn't be enough. Especially if she needed to take the children somewhere that required more than casual clothes.

But that was fine. She could go back to her apartment and get more clothes once she had a handle on what kinds of things she'd be doing. In fact, with the temperature as warm as it had been, she might want to make a run back to her apartment for a bathing suit.

At eleven-thirty, she scampered downstairs to prepare a box of the macaroni and cheese she'd found. But when she made the turn to get into the kitchen she found Lacy already at the weathered table and Mac standing at the counter slathering peanut butter on bread.

"I was just about to make macaroni."

Lacy's face lit up, but Mac said, "We're fine."

"I know you wanted me to spend these first few days getting oriented, but I'm all set now. Ready to handle this job completely. I can make today's lunch."

"I've got lunch, Ms. Swanson."

Finding it curious that he wanted her to call him Mac, yet he had just called her Ms. Swanson, she ambled over to the counter. "Peanut butter sandwiches again?"

"Lacy likes peanut butter."

"I like macaroni too," Lacy said hopefully.

"I'll make that tomorrow," Mac said, dropping another slice of peanut butter bread onto the paper plate and walking it to the table. Lacy frowned and sent Ellie a pleading look.

Ellie half smiled at Lacy. This was it. One of those tests household employees were forced to use. If she pushed him and he barked, she'd know to back off and never push him again. But if she pushed him and he relented, then she'd know there were things about which he could be reasonable.

"It really is no trouble for me to make a box of macaroni."

Mac said, "We're fine—" at the same time that Lacy said, "Please."

The pleading in Lacy's voice, sent Ellie into action. Surely he couldn't resist his daughter? She headed for the stove. "Seriously, Mac. It's no trouble."

Mac pressed his lips together as if to prevent himself from saying something he'd regret. After a few seconds he quietly said, "That's all Ms. Swanson. You may finish your cleaning or take your break. Whatever is on your schedule now. But Lacy and I don't require your services."

Wide-eyed Lacy immediately glanced down at her sandwich. Ellie swallowed and took a step back. She'd just learned two things. He didn't relent, but also this was a man who didn't need to yell to let everybody know he was furious.

Ellie took another step back and prudently said, "I'll be upstairs cleaning."

"Thank you."

Sucking in another breath, Ellie ran upstairs. It had been foolish to anger him—doubly foolish for *him* to get angry over something so trite. But she'd had to push to see how far she could push. Now she knew. Clearly, she'd overstepped her boundaries. And though Mac's volume had been civil, his tone had told her he wasn't pleased.

She wouldn't care if this were just a matter of her job security. As far as she was concerned she could leave tomorrow. But this wasn't about her. This was about Liz and Cain. Liz getting referrals and Cain getting his "in" with Carmichael Incorporated. Surely, she couldn't have blown it over trying to make macaroni?

Not about to go to her room where she'd pace and chastise herself for being stupid, Ellie headed for the laundry room. She set the washer to begin filling, then retrieved the baskets of dirty clothes from the kids' rooms. Seeing that she didn't really have enough for a load, she frowned.

The obvious thing to do would be go into Mac's room and get his dirty clothes to round out the loads. She narrowed her eyes, considering that, and realized that she didn't feel as uncomfortable going into his room today as she had yesterday. All those feelings of attraction she'd been feeling had been snuffed out by the way he'd just treated her.

She almost laughed. Nobody liked being reprimanded, but Mac's behavior might have actually made her time here more tolerable. She wouldn't have to worry about wayward hormones around him anymore.

Her head high, she strode to the master suite door, twisted the knob and marched inside.

A sitting room greeted her. Comfortable white leather chairs sat atop a yellow-, green- and cream-colored Oriental rug on the honey-brown hardwood floors, creating a conversation grouping in front of a fireplace that Ellie would bet had never been used. The room was spotless. There wasn't even a book on the table between the two chairs. It was almost as if no one had ever set foot in this room.

She frowned. Maybe no one had? There were plenty of other places in this house for Mac to read or watch TV. He probably only used this suite to—she swallowed—sleep. In pajama bottoms, with his chest bare and his muscles exposed.

Damn it! She wasn't supposed to be attracted to him.

She gingerly made her way to the bedroom and was surprised when she stepped inside. While her room had a gorgeous black four-poster bed with elaborate bedspread and matching drapes, this room had a simple wooden bed. A queen-size at best. The spread was an almost ugly red-and-yellow print that matched the equally ugly drapes. The area rug beneath the bed was a tortured brown.

She walked to the center of the room and turned in a circle. If she were rich, she'd sue the person who designed this room. As ugly as it was, she was almost afraid to go into the bathroom. But that was where the clothes basket was. In a tidy little cupboard beneath the sink. At least that was where the kids' had been.

With a deep breath for courage, she walked into the bathroom and blinked. It was huge and gorgeous. Turning in a circle again, she took in the shower, complete with an enormous showerhead and six body jets. As in her bathroom, there was a spa tub. An open door in the back of the room revealed a walk-in closet.

Okay. So the house itself wasn't ugly, but Mac's ex-wife's tastes left a lot to be desired.

As she thought the last, she heard the click of the doorknob to the suite and she froze. Oh, great! Here she was standing in the bathroom of his suite like an idiot, obviously snooping! If he hadn't fired her before, he'd probably fire her now. She shot for the cupboard beneath the double sink, hoping she'd find the laundry basket there. As she opened the door, brown wicker greeted her and she just barely had time to yank it out before he walked in.

"Oh, Mr.—Mac." She lowered her head and started for the door. "Just collecting the laundry."

"Actually, I've been looking for you."

She swallowed and glanced up, meeting his gaze. "You have?"

He nodded. "I know you're not a professional nanny. I know you're not even a real maid. But when I give an order you are not to contradict me."

"I didn't realize making peanut butter sandwiches was an order."

Damn it! Why had she said that? Why hadn't she simply said, "Yes, sir," and gotten the hell out of here!

His eyes narrowed at her. "Anything I say and do in this house—especially if it pertains to my children—is an order. Do you understand that?"

This time she did say, "Yes, sir." She actually got halfway to the bedroom door, before something inside her rose up and she couldn't stop herself from turning around. Mac stood by the ugly, ugly, ugly bed. He was gruff. His house was a museum. His daughter was adorable, but subdued. She got up at four o'clock in the morning because she couldn't sleep. Probably because she was nervous. Probably because her dad was so...unbendable.

"All she wanted was a little macaroni."

Mac gaped at her. "Are you questioning me?"

Feeling a strong need to help Lacy, she lifted her chin. "Maybe I'm confused because I'm not a full-time employee," she said, trying to soften the blow. "Maybe I'm confused because I'm also not a parent. But I can't see what difference it would have made to let her eat a little macaroni. She's a kid. She was hungry."

Mac sucked in a breath. Once again Ellie got the impression he was controlling his temper. Fear flooded her. She knew better than to anger a man. Yet, here she was arguing about macaroni. No, she was arguing for Lacy. The kid was a kid, yet in two days Ellie had only seen her playing once. She hadn't been able to choose her own lunch. Something was wrong here!

Finally Mac slowly said, "I was feeding her. And I'll make her macaroni tomorrow."

"But she wanted macaroni today."

Mac squeezed his eyes shut. "Miss Swanson, go do the laundry."

An odd sense of empowerment swelled in Ellie. He was furious with her for questioning him. Yet, he hadn't made a move toward her. He hadn't even yelled.

Still, she wouldn't push her luck.

That afternoon while both kids were napping, Mac paced his office. Nobody—*nobody*—questioned him, yet Ellie hadn't hesitated. He should be furious. He should have instantly fired her for insubordination. Instead, he'd felt a stirring of guilt for denying Lacy what she wanted for lunch and unexpected appreciation that Ellie had a soft spot for his daughter. His appreciation actually got worse when she turned around before leaving and questioned him one more time.

Lacy was a little girl whose mother had abandoned her. Her nanny had refused to move to Coral Gables when they'd run here before Pamela's new movie could be released. She had no aunts and uncles or cousins because Mac was an only child. Her grandparents were jetsetters.

Even Mac felt for her. He'd lived that himself. An only child, dependent upon nannies for support and love. But at least he'd had one stable, consistent nanny. Mrs.

Pomeroy. She was more of a grandmother to him than his grandmother had been. Their bond was so strong that he'd bought her the house in Coral Gables as a retirement gift. It was also why he'd called her when he'd made the decision to hide while Pamela resurrected her career, and Mrs. Pomeroy had suggested he buy the house next to hers. She was here for support, to love his kids, and could even babysit for short spans. But she was eighty years old now. She couldn't be his children's nanny. Not even for three or four weeks while he looked for a new one.

So he knew the value of having a loving nanny. A consistent, stable nanny. If Ellie Swanson checked out, he'd be tempted to offer her anything she wanted to be Lacy and Henry's nanny permanently.

Except for his damned attraction to her.

There they'd stood, in his ugly bedroom—he certainly hoped the people who'd owned the house before him hadn't paid the decorator well—with Ellie being insubordinate, and all he could think of was how close they were to the bed.

It was ridiculous. He didn't know the woman. He could embarrass her or cause her to leave if he made a pass at her. Yet, the pull of attraction he felt to her was so strong, he'd forgotten every one of those good reasons he was supposed to keep his relationship with her purely professional.

He opened his cell phone and checked one more time for messages. If Phil would just get back to him and tell him one way or another about Ellie, then Mac could act. He could either fire her or feel comfortable leaving her alone with his kids and go back to work so he wouldn't have to be around her so much.

But there was no cell phone message from Phil. No incoming call. He was on his own with Ellie Swanson until Phil dug around enough that he was satisfied he knew everything about Ellie's past and could make a recommendation.

CHAPTER FIVE

AT TWO o'clock, Mac came into the kitchen with Lacy and Henry. Ellie looked up from the cookbook she was scouring for recipes.

"I'm taking the kids next door to visit Mrs. Pomeroy."

She frowned at him. "Your neighbor?"

"Yes. She's an old family friend."

Lacy sheepishly said, "I like her."

"Well, of course, you do, sweetie," Ellie said, stooping down to Lacy's level. "You're one of life's very special children who loves everybody."

The little girl grinned happily and Ellie's heart swelled. Lacy was so adorable, and her dad such a grouch, that Ellie had to fight the urge to pull her into her arms and hug her.

Mac directed Lacy away from Ellie toward the hall behind the kitchen. Earlier that day, Ellie had found a side door that led to a walkway that went to the fence and a gate that led to the next house over. So she knew where they were going.

Walking toward the door, he said, "We'll be back before dinner." Then he paused and faced Ellie again. "I'll be grilling hot dogs for supper." He cleared his throat. "And you can...um...make some of that macaroni for us too."

Ellie's mouth fell open in surprise. Their gazes caught and a lightning bolt of electricity sizzled through her. She reminded herself that he was a grouch. She told herself he was out of her league. She reiterated her life plan—that her intuition was always wrong about men, so she was better off staying away from relationships. Yet here she was attracted to a grouchy employer, a man too rich for her, who probably wanted to fire her for questioning him.

But at least he didn't have a temper.

She groaned inwardly as Mac and the kids left the kitchen. Then she slammed the cookbook on the table. It was one thing to be softening her feelings about him as a boss. But finding reasons it was okay to like him—that was wrong! Was she nuts? Seriously? Did she need another lesson about how she always chose the wrong men to be attracted to?

Apparently.

Annoyed with herself, she jogged up the staircase. Mac's bedroom hadn't been a disaster, but it was on her rotation for cleaning. It was better to wipe down the showers and tubs every day than to wait until an employer noticed soap scum. So she headed for the laundry room, where she'd also found cleaning supplies for the upstairs, and went into Mac's room.

The ugly bedroom reminded her that she and Mac were totally different. Scrubbing toilets helped her to remember who she was and where she was and why she shouldn't be attracted to him. By the time she was done in the bathroom she felt much better. Normal. Like a woman who earned her living by the sweat of her brow, who, in spite of her positive attitude, would never set herself up for the embarrassment of falling for an employer and being…well, patted on the head and told she wasn't good enough.

No. No. She knew how the world ran. She wouldn't be bucking that particular system.

Satisfied, she took a dust cloth over the furniture in Mac's room, once again noticing how hideous it was. In a giddy moment, she wondered if poor taste was why he'd dumped his ex-wife, then she spun around, curious. There was not one sign that a woman had ever shared this suite. In fact, that thought actually made sense of the ugly room. Lots of men didn't have any idea how to decorate. If Mac had chosen these things himself, without the assistance of a wife or decorator, then the man wasn't totally gifted after all. He might be rich, good-looking and successful, but he couldn't color coordinate. Plus, if he'd completely redone this bedroom that explained why there wasn't a trace of his ex.

Of course, she hadn't looked in the closet. Surely there was at least a picture.

That roused her curiosity enough that she left her dust cloth on the dresser and tiptoed to the closet. Opening the door, she gasped. The thing was bigger than her apartment! She walked inside, running her hand along the hundreds of dark suits that hung in two long rows. Open shelving held more casual clothing. A back cabinet contained at least five hundred ties. Twenty-three pairs of assorted black shoes lined one row of a three-row shoe rack. The other rows held numerous tennis shoes, different colored dock shoes, various and sundry brown shoes, and ten pairs of navy shoes.

She snooped around, even peeking behind the suits for a door or a box that might contain a few things left behind by his wife. But she found nothing.

Feeling like a fool for being so curious and also realizing that if Mac came in it would appear as if she was casing the joint to rob him, she quickly scrambled out of the closet, grabbed her dust cloth on the way out of the bedroom, stored her cleaning supplies in the laundry room and headed downstairs again.

Through the wall of windows behind the stairway, she saw Mac and the kids returning from their afternoon with the neighbor, and she picked up her pace so she could beat them to the kitchen. The safety zone. The place he expected her to be.

But they didn't come into the kitchen. Using one of the many doors in the house that she couldn't see from behind the stove, they'd entered and probably gone to the playroom or maybe upstairs for the kids' naps.

Walking to the cabinet to retrieve two boxes of macaroni, she shook her head in wonder. Her heart squeezed at the thought that he loved his kids so much he wanted to be their primary caregiver. Her brain was suspicious, thought he was overprotective and worried that he would smother his kids when they got older.

She blew her breath out. Her past too frequently caused her to worry too much about people she didn't know. But maybe that was the real bottom line? She always jumped to conclusions about people she didn't know, speculated about their lives, wondered about their behaviors. But as soon as she got to know someone her confusion stopped. So maybe what she needed to do was get to know Mac?

That made her wince. There were only two problems with that. First, he didn't seem to want her around. Second, she was fighting an attraction for him. She tapped her finger on her cheek. The truth was she'd never met a man she couldn't talk herself out of being attracted to once she spent some alone time with him. It wasn't that she found faults or flaws; it was simply easier to categorize someone as only a friend once she got to know him.

Her phone buzzed and she pulled it from her jeans pocket.

"Hey, Ava."

"Hey, Ellie. What time do you want me over tonight? In time to bring something for dinner?"

"Mac's grilling."

"Oh. That's interesting."

Though she understood Ava's curiosity, Ellie didn't comment. That was one thing she'd always understood. When employed to walk through someone's house, dust their personal things, wash their clothes, a maid could not comment on what she saw. Instead, she said, "How about eight o'clock? Dinner will be over and Mac should be busy upstairs putting the kids to bed."

"Sounds great."

Plus, Ellie was considering spending time with Mac. The best thing to do would be to insinuate herself into dinner somehow. With the worry of Ava popping in at any minute now gone, Ellie could relax and do that. Then this time tomorrow she wouldn't feel any attraction to Mac and she and Mac would probably get along much better.

Mac hadn't needed her help getting the kids or the hot dogs out to the grill that had been set up in a gazebo just beyond the patio. The patio itself had two love-seat-sized sofas with thickly padded seats and glass tables. But the gazebo appeared to have been furnished with the kids in mind. Four-foot walls kept the little ones inside, but also hid the big gas grill and the practical plastic furniture more suitable to children's needs. Comfortable dark-colored chaise lounges created a seating arrangement to the right of the eating area. A leather wet bar probably served the needs of both the gazebo and the patio.

Ellie saw all that when she brought the macaroni and cheese to the table.

"Set it here," Mac said, pointing to one of the huge side arms of the grill, then he went back to tending the sizzling hot dogs, dismissing her.

Ellie's brain scrambled around for a reason to stay. Mac had secured Henry in a highchair and settled Lacy with a coloring book at the comfortable-looking heavy plastic table. There was nothing for her to do. No reason to stay.

But she couldn't leave. This relaxed atmosphere was the perfect place for her and Mac to begin to get to know each other so their relationship would be less strained. Yet she couldn't think of a way to detain herself.

"Everything okay?" Mac asked.

Ellie looked over at him. Think, she told herself. But gazing into his blue eyes, her brain shut down and her hormones kicked in. She wanted to smile, to flirt, to put her arms around his neck and coax him into admitting there was something between them.

Good grief! Why was her imagination so vivid with him? Especially when that was exactly the problem! She *did* want to flirt with him. They had to get to know each other in a more professional way, maybe even become friends, so these crazy feelings inspired by their chemistry would evaporate like the insubstantial vapor they were.

She took a breath. "I thought maybe I could help with the grilling."

"I'm fine."

"Then maybe I could entertain Lacy and Henry while you're busy."

He shot her a look of such distrust that Ellie actually stepped back.

"No."

"I'm really good with kids—"

"You're dismissed, Miss Swanson. May I suggest you tend to your own duties while you have sufficient time to get the housecleaning end of your job in order."

She swallowed. She wanted to call him a pain in the butt, a grouch, a horrible father. But because she was an employee, she couldn't say any of those. Plus, he wasn't a horrible father. If anything, he tried too hard to be a good father and ended up being an overprotective father... She frowned. He'd said he was caring for Lacy and Henry because he was giving her and the kids time to get adjusted to each other. But what if he just plain didn't trust her with his kids?

The thought almost made her gasp. She'd actually considered this already, but had forgotten about it because their damned attraction was so strong it usually pushed every other thought aside.

But she got it now. His secondary purpose for his caring for the kids truly might be to give her and Lacy and Henry time to get adjusted, but the main reason was that he didn't trust her.

"He's a blooming control freak."

Ellie had gone over everything she'd done for Mac and the kids and knew, absolutely knew, the problem was not hers. She'd been helpful, patient, kind, honest, trustworthy. If he still didn't trust her, then *he* had the problem. And because she wasn't telling Ava anything about his kids, his preferences of underwear, even what he stocked in the fridge, she didn't feel she was breaking a confidence.

Particularly since she needed Ava's help understanding him or she'd never last the entire month she'd promised to handle this assignment.

Ava strolled to the weathered table, dropping a stack of files at a place in front of a chair. "Most rich men are control freaks. Cain can be pretty darned demanding himself."

Ellie shook her head, taking the seat beside Ava at the table. "Demanding is one thing. Surrounding your children to keep them from your new nanny is another."

Ava peered over at Ellie. "Why hire a nanny if you won't let your kids near her?"

"Exactly my point."

"That doesn't make any sense."

"Especially since he'll never trust me if he doesn't let me spend time with the kids."

Walking to the kitchen for an apple after putting the kids to bed, Mac heard Ellie's voice. Though he couldn't make out what she'd said, he very clearly heard her speaking and stopped. Was she talking to herself?

"He cooks for them, gets up with Henry at night and Lacy in the morning. He entertains them before he puts them down for their naps and bathes them before bedtime—"

Mac froze. The tone of her voice quite clearly said she was not only displeased with his overbearing behavior about his kids, she was also suspicious.

That wasn't good. Suspicious people went snooping. She wouldn't find anything in this house. But if she got curious enough to go on the Internet, she'd not only discover his ex-wife's identity beyond Mrs. Carmichael, but she'd also realize why Mac was so protective. What she wouldn't guess, though, was that he was still in the process of investigating *her* while his children became accustomed to seeing her in their home, so they'd be comfortable when he went back to work.

Phil probably only needed another day or two. The question was did Phil have that long before Ellie began an investigation of her own?

"He... He..."

"He what?"

Mac's jaw dropped. The voice that nudged Ellie along was new. It took several seconds for that to fully penetrate, when it did his feet took on a life of their own and he propelled himself through the swinging door into the kitchen. She'd let a stranger into his house!

A short, dark-haired woman with black frame glasses sat beside Ellie at the table by the French doors.

"Who is this!"

Ellie's faced turned white in horror. "She's Cain's assistant, Ava."

"And how did she get in?"

Ellie rose. "I let her in. I told you that while Liz is on vacation I have to run Happy Maids. Ava's been doing the office work during the day, but at night I have to approve hours, shift changes and assignments."

Mac tried to stem the roar of his blood through his veins, but he couldn't. This was exactly the kind of mistake that could give away his location.

"Yes, and I also told you that you could leave the house when I'm with the kids."

"But..."

"But what?" he thundered, so afraid for his kids and their sanity that he lost control of his temper. Lacy already didn't sleep through the night. He didn't want her life to become a circus. "You haven't had the kids at all. I told you that the housework was secondary. Why, exactly, couldn't you leave?"

Her already white face paled again. "I'm sorry. You're right. I should have gone to Ava, not had her come to me."

Her apology stopped him cold. He didn't know why he expected her to argue, but when she didn't his anger deflated and he stood there like an idiot. Embarrassed because he'd yelled.

He rubbed his hand along the back of his neck. "I'm sorry that I lost my temper."

"Thank you. But in fairness, you never told me Ava couldn't come in."

He pulled in a breath, counted to ten, then said, "Okay. That was my mistake." He'd thought telling her that she couldn't let anyone know where she was working covered that, but then again by the time he'd set down that stipulation she'd already told her helper at Happy Maids about her assignment. So maybe she felt this woman was grandfathered in or something?

"But I really don't want outsiders in the house. I understand your responsibilities to your boss's company, but I also want my house rules kept. Plus, you're free to leave anytime you don't have charge of the kids. Tomorrow," he said, pointing at Ellie, "you go to her—" he pointed at Ava "—for this meeting."

With that he walked out of the kitchen, his heart pounding and his head beginning to ache. This had been a terrible plan. Hiding in plain sight had sounded so good when Mrs. Pomeroy suggested it, but it was failing. He couldn't use a typical maid company. He'd hired a woman who needed more training and guidance than he had time to give. And that woman was probably growing tired of breaking rules she didn't even know existed.

Still, he didn't blame himself. He blamed the circumstance. His options had been limited.

Walking along the marble floor Mac headed to the main stairway. The cell phone in his pocket rang and he grabbed it. *Phil.* Thank God. He didn't know what he'd do if he had to fire Ellie. He'd used his only option for secrecy when he'd found her. But he did know that one way or another something had to give.

"Can you talk?"

"I'm on my way to my room." He couldn't even go to his office because he had to be available in case Lacy or Henry woke. It was no wonder he was off his game. "So you talk for the two minutes it will take me to get there."

"Okay." Phil paused and Mac heard the sound of his indrawn breath as if what he had to say wasn't good. "I don't know if you're going to like this or not."

"Just spill it. This situation has to change. Even if what you tell me is bad, it only means I start over."

"Okay. Ellie Swanson was a foster kid who ran away. South to Florida where it's warm."

"All of which I know."

"She actually got a job in a pizza shop that was part of a big chain of shops that was growing with leaps and bounds in the South Florida area."

"Oh." So she hadn't spent a lot of time on the streets. That relieved Mac. He hated thinking of her cold and hungry. Which didn't just puzzle him; it angered him. The very fact that he cared about her showed he was beginning to like her and he didn't want to like her. She was insubordinate, pretty, funny…all kinds of things that could be trouble. He wanted her to be a normal employee.

"Yeah. All that's good," Phil said as Mac reached his bedroom.

He walked inside, closed the door behind him and flopped into one of the white leather chairs in the sitting room in front of the bedroom. "So what's bad?"

"I did some digging. Real digging. Talked to friends, employees of the pizza shop who'd been around awhile, neighborhood people, and discovered that the owner of the chain of shops took a special liking to Ellie."

Mac sat up on his chair. "What do you mean 'special liking'?"

"They dated and eventually moved in together."

"Oh." Technically that had no bearing on her ability to be a nanny, so Mac wasn't happy when the news squeezed his heart. It could mean that he was jealous, but since he didn't know her well enough to be jealous, that left option two. He knew what happened when starstruck employees dated bosses who had money and power.

"One employee…a Jeanie Blair…said that Sam Kenward hung around the shop where Ellie worked for a few weeks chatting her up, flirting, being really good to her. He asked her out and he continued to be good to her. Then they moved in together and within a few weeks, Ellie became withdrawn."

Mac sat back in his chair again. "Damn."

"She lived with him for a year. Nobody ever saw a mark on her, but it was fairly common knowledge that he verbally abused her."

Mac pressed a finger to his forehead.

"The reigning rumor is that he hit her once and only once, and she left him."

"Good for her."

"Yeah," Phil agreed wholeheartedly. "She came out of it really well. I don't have specifics on what happened. She never came back to the pizza shop where she worked or contacted her friends."

"Probably because whatever shelter she went to told her that if she contacted anyone they could slip her location to the pizza shop owner."

"Precisely. Anyway, she appears again in employment records when she got a job working for Liz Harper at Happy Maids." Phil chuckled. "From the looks of things she was Harper's first employee."

Which was why Liz trusted her to run her company while she was away.

"I talked with a few of the ladies at Happy Maids and every one of them adores her. They call her Magic."

Mac laughed. "Magic?"

"Yeah, something about her intuition. Anyway her co-workers would trust her with their lives. They call her fierce. They adore her. She babysits for most of them."

Bracing his elbow on the arm of his chair, Mac leaned his face into his hand. "Thanks, Phil."

"So are you keeping her?"

"Actually, I feel like I owe her about eight apologies."

"You've been a real pain in the butt with her, haven't you?"

"Yeah."

"So fix it."

Only someone Mac had known for most of his life could be so bold with him, which was why Mac laughed. "Crawl back under your rock, Phil."

"Call me when you need me."

"I always do." Not because Phil was an employee, because he was an old friend. Phil knew how difficult Mac's life was and knew to keep his secrets. He was discreet when he investigated, and people like Ellie would never know Phil had been investigating them. He might have questioned Ellie's friends and coworkers, but he'd undoubtedly used a great ruse to get information. Her coworkers probably wouldn't even have realized they'd been questioned. Phil was that good.

Mac hung up the phone, paced to his bedroom and opened the drapes to look out at the water. As Phil had said, he had a right to be careful about his kids, but he might have pushed things a bit too far with Ellie. Worse, he'd yelled at her. Sure, he'd backed off once he realized he hadn't told her she couldn't let anyone into his house. But he'd yelled at a maid who'd had a difficult enough life.

Plus, he was attracted to a woman who'd lived the worst-case scenario of getting involved with a boss. He'd have to be a hundred times more sensitive in her presence. He couldn't even say one inappropriate word.

And he somehow had to make this up to her.

CHAPTER SIX

"GOOD morning, Ellie."

Surprised by Mac's unexpectedly happy greeting, Ellie stepped into the kitchen. "Good morning."

"I'm going into the office today."

Though Ellie's mouth dropped open in shock, she noticed that he was wearing a suit and tie. As always, Henry sat in his highchair, beating a rattle on the tray. Lacy sat beside Mac at the table, sneaking shy peeks at Ellie.

"The children are all yours."

That took her shock to astonishment and she had to stifle the urge to say, "Really?" Instead, she said, "Great."

Mac rose, kissed Henry's cheek, then Lacy's, and headed for the door. "I'll see you guys tonight around six." He paused and faced Ellie again. When their eyes met, something new shifted through her. He looked at her totally differently than he had just the day before. It was as if in the past twelve hours something had happened that caused him to trust her.

"I'd like dinner on the table at six when I get home. Lacy can't wait much longer than that to eat. Feel free to give her a decent-sized snack when she wakes up from her afternoon nap."

Then he was off. Ellie got a cup of coffee from the pot that had been brewed and ambled to the table. Dropping to a chair she said, "Well, guys, it looks like we're on our own." She glanced at Lacy. "What would you like to do today?"

Lacy didn't hesitate. "Swim."

"We can do that in the morning. Then this afternoon, what do you say we have a picnic?"

Lacy gasped and put her chubby little hands over her mouth. "A picnic!"

"In the yard."

Lacy bounced out of her seat. "All right!"

She was so excited that Ellie said a silent prayer that she hadn't accidentally stepped over any boundaries. Because the truth was she was as excited as Lacy. She had a month to do all the things she'd always wanted to do with a child. She didn't want to waste a moment.

When Mac came home at three o'clock that afternoon and couldn't find either his children or his nanny, panic filled him. He raced through the house, checking empty rooms and finally saw them when he ran to the French doors to see if they were in the pool.

They weren't in the pool. They were under a tree. In fact, he might not have seen them at all, except something shiny caught the sun and reflected a flash of light strong enough to be noticed.

His loafers made a soft tapping sound as he ran down the stone stairway, then grew silent as he walked across the grass. But he stopped suddenly. Close enough to see Ellie and the kids, but not so close that he'd interrupted them, he gaped at the scene in front of him.

Over shorts and a T-shirt, Lacy wore one of the pretend princess dresses his mother had bought her for her birthday and—he wasn't sure—but he thought his maid was wearing a sheet draped around her and then gathered at the waist to look like a ball gown. Sitting in his baby seat at the edge of the blanket, Henry giggled nonstop, as if thoroughly enjoying the whole thing.

The glimmer of light that had caught his attention came from a mirror Lacy held.

"It's mirror, mirror on the wall, who's the fairest one of all?"

Lacy frowned at Ellie. "What does that mean?"

"Well, the wicked queen was asking the mirror who was the prettiest."

"Why?"

"Because she was jealous of Snow White…a beautiful princess…and she worried that someday everyone would love Snow White more than they loved her." Ellie leaned in closer as if to tell Lacy a secret. "But the truth was the wicked queen wasn't really loved by her subjects."

Lacy's eyes rounded. "Why not?"

"Because she was mean. Snow White was very, very good."

"Oh."

"And do you know what that means?"

Lacy shook her head, sending her soft blond locks bouncing.

"It means that real beauty comes from inside. From how you behave and how you treat people. Not from how you look or what you wear."

Lacy nodded.

"But you'll never have to worry about that," Ellie said, pouring something from a plastic teapot into one of the matching little plastic cups. "You're a very good little girl."

Lacy nodded enthusiastically. "Daddy calls me a princess."

Ellie laughed.

Taking the teacup from Ellie, Lacy asked, "What was the other story?"

"Cinderella?"

"Yes. I like that one better."

"I like that one better too."

Twin arrows lanced Mac's heart. The first arrow was pain. He couldn't believe his ex-wife had never told their daughter simple fairy tales. The second arrow was gratitude. Even after the shabby way he'd treated Ellie the past few days, she wasn't angry or upset. And she was treating his children better than their own mother had.

"What's going on here?" he asked, announcing his presence as he walked over to the blanket spread out on the thick grass.

"We're having a tea party!" Lacy said, springing to her feet. "Do you want some tea?"

"It's actually fruit punch." Ellie picked up one of the tiny cups and poured about two tablespoons of fruit punch into it before handing it to him.

"Thanks." Awkwardness filled him. Not because he'd just lowered himself to a blanket while still dressed in the suit and tie he'd worn to the office. But because he'd so horribly misjudged this woman. She'd had a difficult life. The kind of life he only read about in news magazines. Yet here she sat, playing with his daughter, treating her like a friend or a daughter rather than someone she was employed to care for.

"How did your day go?" He asked the question of Ellie, but Lacy bounced with enthusiasm and joy.

"We swam. We ate pickles. And Ellie told me stories."

"So I heard." He ruffled Lacy's hair. How did a man thank someone for making his child feel normal? He caught Ellie's gaze and she smiled at him as if what she'd done for Lacy had been no big deal.

His heart swelled with something he didn't even dare try to identify. His entire purpose for living was now tied up with these kids. And he suddenly realized that they were his vulnerability. All a woman really had to do was mother his kids and he'd be putty in her hands.

But that was the problem. Pamela's beauty had turned him into a blathering idiot when he'd met her. He'd learned his lesson about getting so wrapped up in one or two of a woman's good traits that he missed the bad ones and found himself tied to the wrong woman forever—if only because of their kids.

He wouldn't put himself through that again. Because of the kids he had to be doubly careful. It didn't matter that the "good" trait of Ellie's that seemed to be snagging his heart was her kindness to his kids. A vulnerability was a vulnerability. A way for Ellie to get power he didn't want her to have. He was too careful to create the same problem twice.

He rose from the blanket. "What do you say we have some Daddy time? You guys stay with Ellie while I change out of my suit, then I'll meet you in the playroom. We'll play that video game you like while Ellie makes dinner."

Lacy bounced up and down. "Okay! This is the best day of my life."

Sadly, Mac knew she was correct. He also knew that even though he would judiciously squelch any and all romantic notions he might get about his temporary housekeeper, he did owe her for everything she'd done for him. Thanks to her, he now had a very good idea of what he'd look for when he began interviewing a new maid/nanny. But more than that, he appreciated how good she was to the kids. Yet, he'd misjudged her.

How did a man make up for any of that?

Halfway up the yard, close to the shimmering pool, he stopped and faced her again. She and Lacy were gathering the tea set and blanket as Henry gurgled happily. "Ellie?"

She stopped. "Yes?"

"Your friend, Ava, can come to the house anytime. I'm sorry I was a little harsh last night. I'm overprotective of the kids, but for good reason."

"Okay."

He turned and headed for the French doors again. Oddly, for the first time in about eight years, he felt his world righting.

The rest of the week passed in a blur for Ellie. Mac worked every day but Sunday. He planned to take the kids out on the ocean for a few hours on Sunday morning and they would spend the afternoon with Mrs. Pomeroy. He suggested that Ellie take the day…really take the day…leave the house, go to her own apartment to check on things, have lunch with friends, even sleep in her own bed and come back early Monday morning.

Ellie didn't need to be told twice. Though she had access to a washer and dryer she hated being in the same clothes all the time. Plus she missed sleeping on her own pillow. She spent the day running around, visiting her friends from A Friend Indeed, doing some shopping and packing a second suitcase.

She returned to Mac's house Monday morning, second suitcase in hand and pillow under her arm. Stepping into the kitchen, she saw Lacy at the table and Mac standing at the counter, holding Henry. She dropped her suitcase to the floor and set her pillow on an available counter.

"Here, let me take him."

Mac didn't hesitate. With another dad, a woman might suspect he was eager to get rid of his slobbering son. But Mac being so quick to give the baby to her was a show of trust. Happiness swelled inside her and the oddest thought occurred to her. If she didn't like her Happy Maids job so much, she really would consider taking this one permanently.

He handed the bubbly baby boy to her. Their arms and hands brushed in the transition and a sprinkle of awareness twinkled through her, reminding her of why she couldn't take this job permanently. Not only did she owe her loyalties to Liz, but also she was attracted to Mac. Lately, with him treating her well, the physical attraction had morphed into a full-blown attraction. She wasn't merely responding to his looks. She liked him.

The second Henry was in her arms, he slapped her, bringing her back to reality.

Mac winced. "I seriously think that means he missed you."

She kissed the baby's cheek. "Well, I missed him." The realization caused her breath to catch. She *had* missed Henry. She'd missed Lacy. She'd missed Mac. She'd been away only twenty-four hours, yet she'd missed this little family. They were definitely staking a claim on her heart. And if she didn't get a hold of these feelings she'd be sad when she left.

Because she would leave. She had to leave. She couldn't risk another mistake with a man that ended in disaster.

Mac ate his breakfast while Ellie fed Henry and chatted with Lacy. Both kids kissed him goodbye, then Lacy spouted a list of things she'd like to do that day. While Henry napped, Ellie and Lacy colored and Lacy filled her in on what they'd done the day Ellie had been away. After that they swam and ate lunch then Lacy and Henry took an afternoon nap, giving Ellie time to take inventory of the house.

The place wasn't any worse for her being away. Mac was very disciplined about replacing toys and tossing dirty clothes into the basket. She ran two loads of laundry, dusted and vacuumed the floors. By the time she was done both kids were awake and ready for a snack.

She fed Henry first then as Lacy ate her fruit and crackers, Ellie began dinner. Just as she was opening the freezer, her cell phone rang.

"Hey, Ava. What's up?"

"Would you mind if I came over a little early today?"

"No. Early's fine."

"Like about four?"

She glanced at the clock on the wall. "Are you at the gate?"

Ava laughed. "Close. But not there yet. I figured I'd call to see if there was anything you needed me to bring you."

"Actually, I forgot to get something out of the freezer for dinner." She winced. "If you really want to help me out, you could stop at Fredrick's and get me some spaghetti sauce and meatballs."

"Sure. Not a problem. See you in about half an hour."

"Great."

True to her word, Ava arrived in a half an hour. She set the steaming container of spaghetti sauce and meatballs on the counter and said hello to Lacy. "Hey, pumpkin."

"Hey, Miss Ava," Lacy said, using the name Ellie had suggested she use when Ava had visited the week before.

"What are you coloring?" Ava asked, sliding onto a seat beside Lacy after giving Ellie the report on the Happy Maids employees' hours and the schedule to sign off on.

"It's Cinderella."

"She's beautiful. Purple is a good color for her."

"Ellie says purple is for royalty."

"Ellie is right," Ava agreed with a laugh.

Ellie handed the signed papers to Ava. "So what's up tonight that you had to come early?"

Ava winced. "Would you believe I have a date?"

"Oh my gosh!" Ellie laughed with glee.

Lacy said, "What's a date?"

"It's when the prince comes to the princess's house, picks her up and takes her to dinner," Ellie explained, using language Lacy could understand.

Lacy's eyes widened. "Wow."

"Yeah, wow is right." Ava rose from her chair. "It's been thirty years since I went on a date. I can't believe I'm going on one now."

"You'll be fine," Ellie said, stifling a laugh. "It's about time you got back into the real world. Your husband's been gone ten years. I can't believe you waited this long to even date."

"Call me picky." Ava organized her papers and turned to go, but she stopped and faced Ellie again. "And you'd do well to follow my example. I've never heard you talk about going on a date."

"I date."

Lacy's eyes widened even further. "You do?"

Ava frowned. "You do?"

"Yes. I've gone out with Norm and Gerry, two of the volunteers from A Friend Indeed."

"Norm and Gerry? Good grief, Ellie! Norm still lives with his mom and if Gerry steps away from his computer long enough to go on a date I doubt that—"

She stopped as Mac stepped into the room.

"Hey, don't stop talking on my account."

Ellie sent Ava a pleading look. Ava's eyes narrowed shrewdly. "I was just on my way out the door."

Lacy said, "Miss Ava has a date."

Mac laughed.

Her gaze on Ellie, Ava said, "Yeah, I've gotta scoot. But we will continue this discussion later. Especially since you and I have to figure out a place to hold the Labor Day picnic for A Friend Indeed." She glanced at Lacy then Mac, letting Ellie know exactly why she wasn't pursuing Ellie's non-dating status. "I'll see you tomorrow."

Grateful Ava had taken the hint and didn't say any more, Ellie spun on Mac. "You're home early."

"And you're using sauce from Fredrick's."

She grimaced. "And meatballs. I forgot to take hamburger out of the freezer. Fredrick's food is always great. I thought if I tossed a salad and added freshly made spaghetti everybody would be happy."

Mac grabbed an apple from the refrigerator and headed out of the kitchen. "That's fine. When you buy things like that just remember to keep the slip from the store. My accountant will reimburse you. I'll be in my office on a conference call. I should be done by six."

"Great."

Ellie breathed a sigh of relief when he was gone. Lacy went back to coloring. Henry slapped his chubby fist on the highchair tray.

Everything was back to normal except the beating of Ellie's heart. Mac always looked ridiculously sexy in his suits and ties, but today the blue shirt he'd worn had picked up the color of his eyes and he looked amazing. With things so comfortable and companionable between them she'd nearly told him that. But she couldn't. Though she wasn't his permanent housekeeper, she was here in a housekeeping capacity. Forget about the fact that she was befriending his children and getting along with him. She was still a servant and she was going to have to do something about this crush of hers.

That night Mac waited until the kids were in bed before he began searching for Ellie. He hoped she hadn't decided to retreat to her room and was glad when he found her sitting on one of the two chaise lounges by the pool.

"Can we talk for a second?"

He asked his question before he walked around the chaise and saw she wasn't sitting in shorts and a T-shirt, having a glass of tea to unwind for the day. She wore a red one-piece bathing suit. Her damp, curling hair indicated she'd been in the pool. And the contented expression on her face reminded him of the expression of a woman after a particularly satisfying love-making session.

He swallowed as visions of satin sheets and palming smooth naked skin filled his brain. But before he could stutter and stammer or even run the hell away, Ellie glanced up from the book she was reading. "Sure. What do you want to talk about?"

Her bathing suit, though a sensual red that revealed the swell of her breasts, was very demure. So why it sent his pulse scrambling, Mac couldn't say. Still, he'd be a blathering idiot to ask her to slip into her cover-up. Instead, he locked his gaze on her face. "You're really doing a great job with the kids."

"Thank you."

"Actually, the reason I came looking for you is that I wanted to thank you for taking such good care of them."

Ellie laughed. "I am the nanny."

He shook his head. "You'd be surprised how many nannies think that just being in the same room with their charges is sufficient." He drew in a breath, sneaked another peek at her swimsuit—the way the taut red material caressed her curves, particularly accenting her tiny waist— then forced his mind back on his purpose for being outside with her.

"You play with the kids. You're especially good for Lacy. I appreciate that."

She ducked her head. "Well, you're welcome."

Mac took a deep breath. Oh, Lord. He hoped he hadn't embarrassed her by looking at her. He was such an idiot. But in his defense she was so beautiful it was damned difficult not to stare.

But he was here on a mission. He'd only used wanting to thank her for taking such good care of his kids as his conversational in. Now that he'd gotten his full report from Phil, it was awkward knowing things about her that she didn't realize he'd been told. Somehow or another he had to get her to tell him about being a foster child, about leaving an abusive relationship, and her close friendship with Liz Harper, so he didn't have to worry that he'd slip up and reveal that he knew any or all of it someday.

He lowered himself to the chaise beside hers. Sitting sideways, so his feet were on the decorative tiles that made up the seating area around the pool, he dropped his clasped hands into the space between his knees. Focused on what he had to say, he ignored the tingling of his fingers. This close to her, every inch of his body jumped to red alert, but his fingers itched to touch her. And that was wrong. And he was an adult. He could ignore one simple attraction.

"You know, we've never really talked."

She peeked at him. "About what?"

"About...you know...about your past."

The confused expression on her face told him this wasn't going well at all. His attraction was making him sound like a starstruck teenager finally alone with his first crush. Which was ridiculous. He was a grown man who had been married. Hell, now that he was free again, he could have his pick of women. Why this one made him stutter was beyond him.

"Like an interview?"

He sucked in a breath and expelled it quickly. "More like a conversation."

She sat up, shifting to sit sideways on her chaise, facing him. The knees of her perfect legs angled only inches away from his. They were so close he could touch her accidentally, satisfy his curiosity about whether her skin was as soft as it looked. But that would be wrong. Wrong. Wrong. Wrong.

"You mean like you would fill me in on a bit of your past and I'd fill you in on a bit of mine?"

Thank God she was thinking like a normal, rational human being and kept the conversation going where he wanted it to go. He could handle telling her a bit of his past. After all, she probably should know some of it in order to properly care for the children.

"Yeah. We should share information about our pasts."

"Okay. I'm really curious about the kids' mom." She grimaced. "Not curious in a gossipy way. But curious in a way that helps me to care for them. I don't want to ac- cidentally say something I shouldn't."

Damn.

He'd hoped she'd start off by talking about herself. Instead she'd led with a question about him. This was what he got for being tongue-tied and stupid just because she was wearing a bathing suit.

"The children's mom left me because having a second child made her career difficult."

Ellie gaped in horror. "Are you kidding?"

His sentiment exactly. "She left when she got pregnant, using the pregnancy months to reestablish herself so that when Henry was born, she could hand him off to me and jump back in again."

"I don't care how liberated you rich people are—that stinks."

He couldn't agree more. Oddly, talking about Pamela had given him back perspective about being attracted to Ellie. He knew the consequences of falling too hard for someone. He had to keep this professional. He couldn't talk in great detail about his ex-wife with a servant. He'd stick with the information she needed to know to do her job. "She visits the kids about once a month—"

Ellie bounced from her chaise indignantly. "Once a month!"

"And I spend the next week answering questions from Lacy. Consider yourself lucky that she's cancelled her visit for July or you would be too."

"How nice of her to let you know in advance," Ellie said sarcastically.

Mac laughed. "I'm sorry. Normally I don't find anything humorous about this situation. But your reaction is a bit funny."

She paced to the pool then back to the side-by-side chaise lounges. Looking down at Mac, she said, "I volunteer for a charity called A Friend Indeed. We work with women with children who are forced to leave abusive homes. I've seen the trauma of a child who misses a parent—even when that parent is abusive. Considering her probable feeling of abandonment, Lacy's fairly well-adjusted."

Finally! The conversation had shifted, and in a brilliant way. Though talking about Lacy, she'd thrown in some pertinent information about herself. Now he could get everything out that he already knew and he could stop tiptoeing around her.

"Well, her mom's been gone eighteen months. Time is healing the wound, helping her adjust," he said, then instantly turned the discussion back to Ellie. "So tell me about this charity. I don't think I've ever heard of them."

"That's because the work they do is confidential."

"I understand. Everything you tell me will be kept in strictest confidence. What, exactly, do they do?"

The mental debate she held about whether to trust him changed her expression at least twice. Finally, he said, "My family's charitable foundation is always looking for worthwhile causes, charities that actually go in the trenches and help people. We know how to be discreet." He caught her gaze. "And we can be very generous. It might be beneficial to A Friend Indeed for you to tell me about them."

Obviously seeing his point, she sucked in a breath and began to pace alongside the pool again. "The charity purchases homes and places abused women in them."

"That's wonderful. How do the women who need help find them?"

"Social Services doesn't exactly recommend a woman leave her husband, but they do provide information about A Friend Indeed to women with kids in high-risk situations."

He frowned. That was the second time she'd mentioned women with children. He knew Ellie had gone to A Friend

Indeed for help. Did this mean she had a child? By forcing her into working for him, was he keeping her away from her own kids?

"How did you get involved with them?"

"I found them." She stopped pacing and faced him, as if suddenly realizing he'd led her to talk about herself, maybe even a part of her past that she wanted to keep hidden.

Feeling the game was up, he smiled sheepishly. "I told you about my wife."

"Because I'm caring for your children. I need to know."

"I'm employing you. Trusting you with those same children. I'd like to know about you."

She licked her lips, drawing Mac's attention to them. Full and smooth, they all but begged a man to kiss her. Now that he'd gotten control of himself, he wouldn't let himself stare too long or want too much, but he couldn't believe a man would be so foolish as to have her and then mistreat her.

"I was…or wanted to be helped by A Friend Indeed." She walked away again, toward the pool, keeping her back to him. "But the night I ran, when I got to the charity, they told me they only take women with kids. Liz happened to be with Ayleen, the group's leader, that night, and she offered me her couch."

That answered his question about her having kids and also explained her fierce loyalty to Cain Nestor's wife.

"And she hired you?"

Ellie nodded then turned suddenly. "So what does your wife do for a living that's so important that she can only see her kids once a month?"

He stifled a sigh. She wasn't going to tell him about the pizza shop owner. Wasn't going to share her fears or the struggle to get back to a good place in life. And both of those were too personal for him to push her into talking about them.

Of course, maybe if he answered a few more questions about Pamela, Ellie would answer a few more personal questions about her life.

He caught her gaze. "It's not what she does. It's where she lives. California."

Ellie's pretty mouth dropped open. "California!" She blinked a few times then she said, "Oh, my gosh! She's on TV or something, isn't she?"

"Or something."

His vague answer brought a spark of fire to Ellie's amber eyes. "Oh, I get it. I can tell you about me, but you're not going to give me any more information than you have to."

He was tempted to debate that. Not only had he revealed much, much more than she had, but also she hadn't really told him about herself. Thanks to Phil, he knew there was more. *Lots* more. But he also understood what she was saying. Her admissions were difficult. His was merely embarrassing. Sad for his children, but not gut-wrenching, the way hers had been. He had to tell her everything, make himself vulnerable, if he wanted her to share with him.

"Okay. She was a movie star. She's trying to edge her way into a comeback." He rose from his chaise and walked over to her. "Nothing seriously awful happened in our marriage. We fell out of love. She wanted her career back. She deserted her kids. But she didn't abuse them. She isn't one of Satan's minions. She's a selfish, narcissistic pain in the ass, but we survived her leaving. My big secret and the reason I don't talk about this is that we're sort of in hiding."

"Sort of?"

He got close enough to smell her soft scent, tempting fate because they were in one of those odd positions of life. They were too attracted to be friends, but he had to trust her and she had to trust him if this situation was to work. They were both pushing. And his admissions, though less serious, weren't any easier than hers. So why not get a tiny reward? Why not step close to the fire?

"Mrs. Pomeroy was my nanny. She called me when this house came on the market and suggested that we hide in plain sight. Our neighbors know who we are. But when Pamela's movie comes out next month, the paparazzi who come looking for us will go first to the family mansion in Atlanta. By the time they realize we're not there and investigate where we've moved, the noise Pamela tries to create might be over. If it's not, we'll move again."

Her big brown eyes captured his, holding his gaze. She studied him, as if trying to figure out if he were being honest. A few seconds stretched into a minute, and before common sense had time to remind him that they couldn't be this close for this long without resurrecting their chemistry, suddenly the air between them crackled with life and energy. His blood heated. His fingers itched to sink into her curling hair. His mouth longed to taste her. And though he knew nothing could ever come of this, he once again stepped closer to the fire.

Ellie took a step back, away from the powerful pull of him. She longed to run her fingers through his hair, touch his cheek, kiss his wonderful mouth. She told herself that he was off-limits. Yet for some reason or another, her body wasn't listening to her common sense tonight.

She took another step back. "Your ex-wife is Pamela Rose?"

He nodded.

"Wow." She wasn't surprised by the fact that his ex-wife had been a starlet. He was the kind of guy who'd attract a starlet. What wowed her was that she was here—in his company, living in a mansion. Sometimes she forgot just how rich and powerful he was. And he was confiding in her.

"Now, do you see why we're in hiding?"

"I guess."

He chuckled. "You guess?"

"Come on, Mac. A rich guy like you has to have an army of public relations people at your disposal. Surely, they could dispel a few rumors."

"I'm not worried about rumors. I'm worried about pictures. Because of my family's money, I grew up with bodyguards, silent alarms and restrictions on where I could go and what I could do. But I still had a measure of privacy. Once I married Pam, everything changed. When your picture gets on the front page of enough tabloids, people start to recognize you. I don't want that to happen to my kids. So I have to keep them away from the paparazzi, so they're not recognizable, because that makes them targets for extortionists and kidnappers."

She'd never thought of that. If no one knew what Mac's kids looked like, they could walk the streets or go to the beach, without anyone suspecting who they were and seeing potential ransom amounts instead of two beautiful children.

"True."

"Which is why I don't want the kids off the grounds."

She shook her head. "But that's exactly the opposite of what you're trying to accomplish."

"Not really."

"Yes. *Really.* You're supposed to be hiding in plain sight but in case you haven't noticed, you're a prisoner in your own house."

"It's the price we pay for my stupidity in making such a poor choice for a mate."

Her heart thumped at his admission that he'd made a bad choice in his first marriage. He really wasn't in love with his ex-wife anymore. And he really was attracted to her. So much so that he couldn't keep his eyes off her. They held her gaze when she stood close, followed her when she paced. And now he was confiding in her. Part of her longed to step closer to take what it seemed he was trying to offer. The other part knew they were a bad match. This very conversation proved it. He was a man who felt he needed to hide. She was a woman who'd only recently learned how to live without hiding.

She stepped away from him and focused on the kids. She knew what it was like to be a prisoner. She also knew that she'd gone overboard before Liz had talked her into getting out into the world beyond simply working. It had taken Liz an entire year to lure her into restaurants and help her to make friends at A Friend Indeed. And her life was better, richer for it.

She'd spent a lot of unnecessary time in her self-imposed prison. And perhaps he and his kids were too.

"I think you're crazy. Hiding in plain sight means you move to a place where no one expects you to be so that when they hear your name, even if they recognize it, they don't connect you to the 'billionaire' Mac Carmichael because they expect the billionaire Mac Carmichael to be under lock and key, and certainly not out and about in their neighborhood."

"That's ridiculous."

"Really? Because the way I see it, if there have never been pictures of your kids, the average person couldn't possibly know who they are. It's not like they wear a sign that says, 'My dad's a billionaire'."

He laughed, so Ellie pressed her point home. "Even *your* face isn't that recognizable. Everyone knows who you are when you're connected to your companies, like giving a press conference. But put on a pair of shorts and a fishing hat and walk into the mall and I'll bet nobody knows you."

At first Mac laughed, then he realized she wasn't kidding and his laughter stopped. "You're serious?"

"Yes. As long as no one knows what your kids look like there's no reason to hide them."

He shook his head. "Going out hoping that no one knows who we are would be a dangerous way to live. All it takes is one person to recognize even one of us for pictures to be taken and the entire world to know."

"I doubt it. Most people don't read *Forbes* or *Fortune*. And those are the only places your name and picture appear regularly."

"Right. The second I pull out a credit card the clerk knows my name."

"And you think a clerk at the mall is going to know who Mac Carmichael is?" She laughed gaily. "Come on. You're only famous in your own circle. Store clerks won't know you. Neither will the kid at the food court."

He frowned, seeing her point.

Her eyes sparkled with mischief when she caught his gaze. "Let's do an experiment. Let's take the kids to the mall tomorrow night. We'll go to a fast food restaurant and walk through a few stores. Lacy will probably die of happiness and you'll see that you don't have to be a prisoner."

With her voice light with merriment and her eyes shining, it was so tempting to Mac to lean into her, brush a kiss across her lips, tease her into taking his side. So he stepped back, away from temptation, into his comfort zone.

Obviously thinking he'd stepped away because he disagreed, she caught his arm. "Please. Even if you never want to do it again, do it once. For Lacy. She'd love this."

A storm of electricity burst through him, like lightning penetrating thick storm clouds. He stared into her wise brown eyes and didn't see the corresponding attraction he knew she felt. Instead, her earnest expression told him she really was bartering for the day out for his daughter. Appreciation rose up in him, battling the sexual needs coursing through him. He had a choice: say he'd think about it and run like hell to get away from temptation. Or stay. Take the conversation away from Lacy and to him. What he wanted from her. What he needed. What it could mean for them, if he were that free. That trusting.

He swallowed as intimate pictures formed in his brain, surprising him with their simplicity and intensity. He wanted this woman in a way he hadn't wanted a woman in a long, long time. Not just sexually, but intimately. There was definitely a difference. A frightening difference.

She gasped as if suddenly thinking of something. "You've probably never been to the mall." She laughed merrily. "Trust me. Lacy will love it. And I swear I'll guide you along the whole way."

Trust her. That was the problem. He wanted to trust her. But he knew he couldn't. At least not with his heart. But maybe the best way to get over his desire would be to get to know her as a normal person. Take her up on her offer with Lacy. Not to acquiesce to what she wanted, but to put her into the position of nanny more firmly. Surely he could risk one day. Especially if he stationed bodyguards in the mall.

"Should I come home early for this?"

Her eyes lit with joy. "Really? You're going to do it?"

"Sure."

"You don't have to come home early. Just be ready to put on a pair of jeans and a T-shirt when you get home." She headed for the house but faced him again and smiled. "And we'll take the suburban. That's the car that will attract the least attention."

"If we really wanted to blend, we should take yours."

That seemed to tickle her and she laughed with delight. "You probably couldn't fit into the front seat."

Then she turned and walked up the stairs, into the house. Mac lowered himself to one of the chaise lounges. He couldn't believe he'd just agreed to a trip to the mall, but he had. Partially because she was right: Lacy would love it. Partially because it was simply fun to see Ellie so happy, so full of life. She was the kind of woman who would make a happy home. The kind of woman any man would want for a wife.

He ran his hand down his face again, wishing he'd met her before his ex-wife had destroyed his faith in people.

And before a former boss had destroyed hers.

CHAPTER SEVEN

SITTING in the driver's seat of the suburban, wearing a yellow fishing hat, one of his golf shirts and cutoff jean shorts, Mac felt like a damned fool.

"This is a stupid idea."

Ellie peeked over at him and, God help him, she couldn't stop her eyes from wandering up to the yellow hat. She giggled.

He scowled. "A *very* stupid idea."

"Not really."

Her voice was soft and placating, causing him to suspect she was lying. But she smiled, and even in the semi-dark garage, the car seemed to light up.

"The purpose of the hat is for you to blend in."

"By looking like an idiot?"

"You look like an average guy going to the mall with his kids."

"Average guys don't wear stupid hats and look ridiculous."

"Of course they do." She peeked over at him again. "How long has it been since you've been in the real world? Men wear baseball caps backwards and knit hats in the summer. Hats are the big way men make their fashion statements."

He snatched the offending yellow hat off his head. "Rappers wear knit caps and goofballs wear their baseball caps backwards. Mostly to cover bald spots. But my hair is perfectly fine as it is."

In the booster seat in the back Lacy giggled. "Not really, Daddy."

He looked in the mirror. The hat had reshaped his hair so that portions were sticking out at odd angles. He flattened it down with his hand. "There. Now, let's go."

He'd be canceling this trip right now if Lacy's eyes hadn't lit with absolute astonishment when Ellie announced that they were going to the mall. Hell, why not get to the real bottom line? They wouldn't be going to the mall at all if he didn't feel like hell for treating Ellie harshly when she'd already had a difficult enough life.

He was a goofball. And maybe he *should* put on the yellow hat.

Mostly because he knew this wasn't the end of it. He might not let Ellie taunt him into another foolish trip, but he would sometimes buckle under about stupid things for Lacy. She was a kid and he wanted her to have some semblance of a life. He most certainly wanted her to have fun. And going to the mall with her dad—as long as she stayed with her dad—wouldn't be dangerous. Particularly since he had called Phil and company and told them to be at the mall at seven o'clock. They weren't to wear dark suits with their shoulder harnesses exposed so everyone around could see they had a gun, but were to blend in.

He glanced at the offending yellow hat on the compartment between him and Ellie. If hats were a way to blend, then Phil should be the one wearing this one.

"The first thing we're going to do is go to the food court," Ellie said, turning on the front seat of the Suburban so she could speak to Lacy and Henry.

Mac hid a grin. He had to admit he loved the way she kept Henry in the loop. The baby probably didn't understand much beyond Daddy, eat and nap, but when Ellie spoke he stared at her with rapt fascination.

"We'll eat a hamburger and fries and then I understand there are three children's stores on the first level."

Lacy gasped. "Can I get a princess dress?"

Ellie glanced at him and he caught Lacy's gaze in the rearview mirror. "Let's wait and see what's in the store."

"Ah, Dad!"

"Princess dresses are typically found in toy stores," Ellie jumped in, saving him. "They aren't normal clothes. They're special. When you put on a princess dress your imagination soars and you become anyone you want. At school, you have to be yourself so that you remember everything you learn and some of the things we might buy tonight would be for school."

Lacy nodded sagely as Mac drove them to the mall. Hundreds of multicolored cars were parked in long, rather organized rows. At first glance, he didn't see an empty space. And he hadn't instructed Phil to arrange for one.

Of course, that would have defeated the purpose of the entire trip. If a bodyguard arranges with mall management to have orange cones in a front row spot until you arrive so you can be hustled in, everybody pretty much knows you're somebody important. Pamela had loved that.

But this trip was about seeing if they could blend, seeing if they could every once in a while take Lacy out into the world and let her observe how real people lived. It was about seeing if maybe—if they kept her profile low-key enough and if he secretly placed bodyguards inconspicuously around her—maybe she could go to the mall with her friends when she was in her teens.

"Where to?"

"Just drive around until we find an open space."

He nodded and they circled the mall twice, not finding a space close enough that they didn't have to walk a distance to get into an entrance. By the fourth pass, he decided he would carry Lacy and Ellie could carry Henry, because they weren't going to find a closer spot.

They stepped into the noisy mall and Ellie directed him to the right. "It's a bit of a walk, but the food court is this way."

Mac couldn't help it; his head twisted from side to side, taking in the people as well as the building. Ellie was right. Real people did sometimes dress like goofballs. The atmosphere was almost like that of a carnival. They found the food court where Mac took a quick look around and saw Phil and three of his employees milling about. Phil wore a suit, but it was older and he let his jacket hang off the back of a white plastic chair where he sat eating a hamburger. Two of the other guards wore jeans and T-shirts. The third guy wore shorts and by damned if he wasn't wearing a khaki fishing hat.

Okay, so maybe Ellie hadn't been too far off the mark about the ugly hat.

Lacy ordered something called a "happy meal" and Mac and Ellie ordered salads. Then Ellie added a small order of fries for Henry.

Though he'd never been to a mall, Mac had eaten fast food before. He hadn't been particularly impressed, but for some reason or another, the scents from the food in this mall were amazing. Everything smelled delicious. When his stomach rumbled, he quickly added two hamburgers to his salad.

When they were finished eating, Ellie directed them to the three stores stocked with children's clothing. Lacy ran in, her mouth open with shock, her face registering pure, unadulterated feminine pleasure.

He leaned over to Ellie and said, "This is going to cost me a pretty penny."

Ellie gaped in horror. "No! You don't let her buy everything she wants. You tell her she can have two things."

Mac frowned. "Two things? There are hundreds of things in here."

"And she'll never possibly be able to use them all. She already has a closet full of clothes. Plus, if you buy her everything she wants, she'll have too much to appreciate it."

"But she's never shopped on her own before."

"Which makes this a perfect time for her to learn to shop with care. Not to be greedy. To appreciate what she has."

"She's only six."

Ellie shook her head and laughed. "Yes. Old enough to understand the lesson and young enough that you can still have the hope that the lesson will stick."

Mac pulled in a doubtful breath. "Okay. We'll play it your way."

He turned to catch up with Lacy, who was skipping up the aisle of the colorful specialty shop, but Ellie caught his arm. Pinpricks of awareness raced to his shoulder, across his chest and down to his stomach. She looked beautiful in her light blue T-shirt and white shorts. Her legs were long and tan, her golden hair bouncy and shiny.

"She'll thank you for this when she's older. She won't see the world as a place to take. And if we carry this lesson a bit further we might also teach her that she should also give, not always get."

He caught the gaze of his housekeeper, knowing she'd been a foster kid, knowing someone had abused her, knowing she'd worked her way from nothing and still she had the common sense and intelligence of a true lady.

Something warm squeezed his heart. Not only was she a lady, but she wanted his daughter to be a lady too. That was all any father really wanted. A daughter who appreciated what she had, gave as much as she got and acted like a lady.

"Have I told you thank you for the suggestion to come to the mall?"

"Mostly you groused about the hat."

"Well, thank you." A sudden instinct to lean in and kiss her rose up in him. It was so strong that if they hadn't been in a public place he sincerely doubted he would have been able to resist it.

But they were in a public place and she was his employee. And she'd been abused by a former boss. She'd trusted an employer and he'd hurt her in the worst possible way. No matter what Mac wanted, no matter how tempted, no matter how much he told himself he would be different, he couldn't forget her needs, her fear. He had to squelch any romantic urges.

After ten minutes of Lacy rummaging through the racks, Ellie broke the news that she could choose two things.

Lacy turned her pretty blue eyes up to her father. "Can't I have more?"

"Why do you need more?" Mac asked, taking his cue from Ellie who had told him that Lacy probably wouldn't use everything she'd want to buy.

"Because they're all so pretty."

"And you already have lots of pretty clothes."

She stuck out her lower lip. "But I want these!"

Mac's heart rate sped up. His soul filled with remorse. He wanted to give Lacy everything she wanted. He knew it was wrong. He knew everything Ellie said was right. But, damn it, Lacy was his little girl. He was rich. She *should* have everything she wanted!

"Lacy?" Ellie called to the little girl who looked on the verge of tears. "You don't want to buy everything here. You might not want to buy anything here at all. We have two other stores to go to. What if the dresses in those stores are prettier?"

Lacy's face transformed from sulking to confusion. "There are more stores?"

"Three. Remember?" She put her hand on Lacy's shoulder and guided her out of the store. "You don't simply want to buy everything. You want to buy the best, the prettiest. In the next store, I'll show you how to look for something that suits the color of your eyes. We're also going to think about where you'll wear what you buy. You may see that you actually have nowhere to wear some things." She shrugged. "So there's no point to buying them."

Lacy's face brightened with understanding. "Okay."

She skipped toward the entrance where two of Phil's guys sat on a bench pretending to be holding a conversation. Knowing Lacy was safe, Mac turned to Ellie. "There's some secret woman code in what you told her, right?"

She laughed. "No. Just common sense."

They trooped to the second store. Lacy checked out the racks in a more judicious way. Mac had taken the baby so Ellie could help her, and he strolled down a nearby aisle.

He'd never considered the time or money that went into purchasing things for his children. Mrs. Devlin had done all that. But now he didn't have a nanny and he seriously wondered if there weren't things he should be buying.

After a few minutes, they found the third store. Lacy and Ellie went their way and Mac walked the aisles, looking at clothes for Henry, wondering if he needed new things and even what size he wore. Lacy chose a pair of capris with a new blouse and a brightly colored sundress.

"Two outfits," Ellie explained, telling Mac with her expression that he shouldn't question that.

"That's great. They're very… pretty," he said at the last second because he wasn't sure what to say.

Ellie laughed. "We might want to pick up a pack or two of diapers," she said as they approached the checkout lane.

Mac pulled in a breath. "I wondered. We've been without a nanny for a while. You've worked for us almost two weeks and Mrs. Devlin left the week before that. Even if we had a stockpile of diapers, Henry has to be going through them fairly quickly."

Ellie chose the diapers and put them on the counter with Lacy's things.

"Does he need any clothes?"

Ellie shook her head. "No, he's fine for a few months. Then you may have to shop."

"By then I hope to have a real nanny."

A shadow passed over Ellie's face and Mac instantly regretted his comment. "I didn't mean to sound as if we'll be relieved when you go. It's more about getting our lives back to normal."

She glanced away. "I understand."

But he didn't think she did understand. Her voice was soft, sad, as if she was accustomed to being unwanted, asked to leave. She turned and walked out of the store, Lacy chattering happily on her heels.

Mac hung back, cursing in his head for his stupidity. He didn't want her to leave. He wanted to keep her. But how could he? How could he ask her to give up a life she was building as an executive in a new company to become his permanent nanny? Worse, if she stayed too long, he knew he wouldn't be able to resist her. Some moonlit night or sunny afternoon he'd kiss her...and he'd be no better than the boss who seduced her and then abused her.

So she couldn't stay.

But he also wouldn't let her spend the night feeling badly. As soon as the kids were in bed, Mac intended to explain how much he appreciated her, how much he wished he could keep her and maybe even why he couldn't.

CHAPTER EIGHT

AFTER Mac had put the kids to bed, Ellie stepped out of the French doors onto the steps that would take her to the gazebo. She wasn't sure what she was doing. She had no idea what she would say. But even though they'd had a great trip to the mall, she'd seen the bodyguards. She'd also sensed Mac's fear. He might have taken Lacy and Henry out that night, but she sincerely doubted he'd do it again.

The thought that he couldn't see that they didn't have to live in a prison wouldn't let her alone. She had lived that prison. Plus, she was trained to help women transition out of abusive homes, and everything about this family reminded her of the families she dealt with at A Friend Indeed. She'd be shirking her duties as A Friend Indeed volunteer if she didn't try to help him.

She tripped down the yellow steps and strolled past the pool. Cool night air swirled around her, indicating that a storm was probably rolling in.

Passing the patio beyond the pool, she walked along the stone path to the gazebo where she paused just in front of the two steps that would take her inside, to where Mac sat.

When she entered the gazebo he'd either think it was a coincidence that they'd gone to the same place, or he'd know she'd watched him come out here and followed him.

Which was bad on so many levels. The only way she could comfort herself was to remind herself that she was trained to help spouses transition out of bad relationships. And if he needed her...

She took the two steps up into the gazebo.

Soft music greeted her. She didn't recognize it. It wasn't pop or rock or even a well-known classical song. Soft and mellow, it reminded her of a blues melody.

"Hey."

He glanced up at her and rose from the chaise lounge. "Hey."

Showing him the baby monitor, she said, "I brought this so we could have a few minutes to talk."

His eyes narrowed. "You want to talk?"

She nodded.

"So do I."

"Then it looks like we're on the same wavelength. You go first."

"No. You go first."

"All right. I thought the trip to the mall went very well tonight, but I sense that you weren't comfortable and you might not do it again."

"Ellie, this isn't a matter of me being uncomfortable. It's a matter of safety."

"I understand that, but you can't keep your kids in a bubble forever."

"I won't."

She laughed lightly. "You'll try."

"Of course, I'll try. I'm a father. It's what we do."

"But without a mom to argue the other side for your kids, you're always going to win."

This time he laughed. "Actually, that's what I wanted to talk about with you."

"Really?"

"Yes. Tonight when I mentioned getting a permanent nanny, you seemed to get really sad. I wanted you to know that if you truly wanted the job, I'd hire you in a heartbeat. Nobody's ever been as kind to Lacy. She adores you."

Ellie fought the tears that wanted to form in her eyes. Lacy was such an adorable little girl that Ellie couldn't believe a mother could abandon her. But soon Ellie would also abandon her. "I like her too."

"But?"

"But I have a job that I love."

He smiled ruefully. "That's exactly what I told myself when I saw the sad expression come to your face. You might love my kids, but you also love your Happy Maids job. And you're working your way up the corporate ladder. You're getting experience in management that will lead to security."

She straightened her shoulders, obviously proud of her accomplishments. "I am."

"So you need to stay where you are."

She nodded. "Yes."

"Which means someday I won't be your boss."

She frowned, wondering what the heck that had to do with anything. She raised her eyes until she could meet his gaze. When she did she saw the same curiosity in his expression that she felt twinkle through her every time they got close enough to touch. The sensation got worse every day because every day they seemed to grow closer emotionally.

He'd held his curiosity at bay because of their employment situation, but tonight they'd basically set it in stone that soon she wouldn't be his employee.

She swallowed. She'd never thought of that and from the look on his face he hadn't either—until tonight. Tonight with a gentle rumble of thunder mixing and mingling with the soft music filling the gazebo, and a sweet-scented breeze wafting around them, they'd made the connection that they didn't have to ignore their attraction.

The music shifted from a spirited blues song to something soft and wistful and he stepped toward her. "I can't remember the last time I danced. I'm very adept at dodging would-be partners at charity events. But tonight is different. Tonight I'm in the mood." He caught her gaze. "Want to dance?"

His blue eyes were soft and honest and though she knew it was foolish considering that she was still in his employ, still living under his roof, something inside her couldn't say no. She wanted this. She wanted to feel his arms around her, his chest pressed against hers, his chin resting on the top of her head. Nothing would come of it. At least not while she was in his employ. She was very strong when it came to holding the line in her relationships. Plus, he was as taken as she was by their attraction, but she had seen him pull back several times. Surely, she could trust him to pull back again, if things got too heated.

She smiled and held out her hand. He pulled her into his embrace and the whole world softened. It was everything she could do not to close her eyes and melt against him.

He nudged her a little closer.

The muscles she held so stiffly ached in protest, so she relaxed a bit.

He pulled her closer still.

And her body relented. Doing what her head had been so determined to stop, she melted against him.

"That's nice."

"Yes." Her voice was nothing but a thready whisper that wove into the sweet music drifting around them. The

remnants of distant thunder continued to grumble over-
head, matching the muted warnings whispering through
her brain. *Be careful. Be careful. Be careful.*

But the warnings were soft, and as she swayed to the
song, nestled against a man she was coming to care for,
they grew quieter and quieter, mitigated by the other side
of the argument running through her brain. Mac wasn't
a man who would hurt her. She'd seen his worst when he
discovered Ava in his kitchen. He'd also apologized, not
rationalized that no matter what her explanation she was
somehow at fault, as Sam would have done.

Thinking about Sam sent a burst of fear skittering
through her, but as quickly as it manifested, it shimmied
into nothing. Sam and Mac were nothing alike. In fact,
she'd venture to say they were polar opposites.

Oddly, that realization scared her even more. The de-
fenses that had been protecting her, the fears that saved her
from another mistake, were being silenced around Mac.
Her instincts were screaming that that was because Mac
was a good man. But was he? How could she say for sure
when she'd only known him a few weeks?

Suddenly Ellie realized they were no longer dancing.
The music still drifted around them but they stood perfectly still. Her hand tucked in his. His arm comfortable
at her waist. Their chests a breath away from each other.
Their eyes locked.

"I won't hurt you."

Had he read her mind? Was she that transparent?

She whispered, "I know."

"So don't be afraid."

"I'm trying."

"That's all I ask."

She expected him to pull her close again. Instead, he leaned down and brushed his lips across hers. A light, wistful sweep of his mouth against hers. A promise more than a real kiss.

Mac stepped back, releasing her. "You might want to go back inside now."

She continued to hold his gaze. Sincerity and stability were the two most important things to her right now and his perfect blue eyes were telling her she could trust him.

Then his gaze dropped to her mouth and as seconds ticked away, the expression in his eyes shifted from soft to sexually charged. He was a good man, but he was also a man who wanted her.

Her heart stuttered in her chest. She wasn't sure how to deal with that or even if she could. Part of her simply wanted to relent and do what they both wanted to do. The other part was afraid. She'd been burned once. No matter how many times she told herself he was different, he wouldn't hurt her, she knew her instincts about men had been wrong before. They'd told her she could trust Sam. She knew she had to be strong, smart.

And the smart thing right now would be to follow his suggestion and leave.

She turned and ran out of the gazebo, up the soft grass, along the cool tiles and up the stone stairs to the kitchen. In her room, she stood by the window, staring out at the gazebo, knowing he sat in there alone.

Mac fell into the chaise lounge again. He squeezed his eyes shut, trying not to think of that kiss. Unfortunately, when he shoved his mind off the kiss it jumped to Ellie being abused. When he shifted his mind off that, he envisioned her younger, alone and frightened on the streets, running from a foster home. He couldn't handle the thought of Ellie being alone. He tried not to imagine how it felt to live on the streets as Phil had said she had done. He tried to ignore the swell of protectiveness that rose up in him.

Especially when a soft voice reminded him that he'd opened a door tonight that he probably shouldn't have opened. She'd already escaped several bad situations, and if he got involved with her he would be taking her directly into another. She wouldn't be on the streets or living with an abusive man, but she'd be locked in what she so clearly described as a private prison. If what he felt for her blossomed into love and they married, she'd live here, behind a gate. If she did leave the house, she'd be surrounded by bodyguards.

He cursed and began to pace. What was wrong with him? He knew better than to start something with her. She was too sweet, too innocent. He should have kept his hands off her. Not because she wasn't pretty enough or even because she wasn't special, but because she *was* special. Honest. Genuine. His life would crush her—or at the very least crush her spirit.

But what if it didn't? What if beneath all that sweetness was a layer of steel? What if her life had made her strong? And what if she chose him? What if she entered this life of his with her eyes wide-open? Ready to handle whatever came their way. Ready to mother his kids and love him.

Thunder rumbled closer this time, as if reminding him that wishful thinking was dangerous.

The only way she could come into his life, eyes open, fully prepared, would be if he really did let her choose. If he backed off and let her make the next move.

CHAPTER NINE

AFTER a nearly sleepless night, Ellie woke at four. Refusing to let herself think about what had happened in the gazebo, she sauntered downstairs, but Lacy wasn't at the weathered table. So she made a pot of coffee and sipped at three cups, waiting to make Lacy's breakfast, but to her complete joy Henry's six-thirty wake-up call came before Lacy woke.

Finally, closer to seven, the little girl tripped into the kitchen, rubbing her eyes sleepily. "Hi."

"Hey, pumpkin." Ellie juggled Henry on her lap. "You must be really hungry after that long sleep."

"Yeah." Bear under her arm, Lacy ambled to the table.

"Who had a really long sleep?" Mac walked into the room, dressed, as always, in a dark suit. Today he wore a white shirt and aqua tie. He couldn't have been more handsome to Ellie if he'd tried.

Then she remembered he'd kissed her.

She caught his gaze and for several seconds they simply stared at each other. So much had happened between them the night before and yet nothing had really happened. He'd brushed his lips across hers. That was all. It hardly counted as a kiss.

So why was her heart beating erratically at just the memory? Why did her breath shiver through her chest? Why couldn't she look away?

"Lacy had a really long sleep," she said, working to make her voice sound normal. "She just woke up."

Mac's gaze swung to his daughter. "Really?"

She grinned at him and nodded.

He strode to the table. "Well, that's cause for celebration." He glanced at his watch as if gauging the time he had and turned to Ellie. "Can you make pancakes?"

Glad to have both of their minds off that kiss, Ellie happily said, "Absolutely."

Henry screeched.

Mac took him from Ellie's lap. "I haven't forgotten you." He kissed his cheek noisily. "Has he eaten yet?"

"Yes. Henry woke a little before Lacy did. I bathed him and fed him." She surreptitiously caught Mac's gaze again. "So you're safe."

Mac laughed and hugged his son.

Something warm and soft floated through Ellie. She didn't have to worry that he'd ravish her in front of his kids. He was a dad and though he liked Ellie, there was propriety to consider. She also didn't have to worry that he'd treat her any differently. In fact, they were behaving as they always did. Except today she wasn't on the outside looking in. That kiss the night before had brought her into the world she'd only been working in yesterday. Today she was part of the family. A *normal* family. Everything she'd always dreamed of. Everything other people had but she'd always believed was just beyond her reach was suddenly hers.

Tears filled her eyes and she turned away, busying herself with the pancakes as Mac entertained the children.

That was foolish, dangerous thinking. This wasn't hers. It wasn't her life. She wasn't even really their maid. She was a stand-in. Temporary help.

But what about that kiss?

Beating the pancake batter, she squeezed her eyes shut. It wasn't really a kiss. It was only a brush.

No. It was more like a question.

Is this right?

Do you want this?

The tears filling her eyes threatened to spill over. Did she want this? Of course, she wanted this. That wasn't the question. The question was…was it right? Would she get hurt?

Didn't she always get her hopes up and get hurt?

Yes.

That was why she was strong. Why she looked before she leaped.

She sucked in a breath, forced her tears to stop, made the pancakes and served them to this happy little family the way a good maid was supposed to. Though she knew Mac wouldn't have protested if she'd served herself a pancake and sat at the table with him and his children, she resisted temptation. She was too smart to wish for something she couldn't have.

She helped Henry wave goodbye to Mac as he left for work then dressed Lacy in something pretty. And fought not to think about how well she fit, how much her intuition screamed that she belonged here.

When Ava arrived that afternoon, Lacy and Henry were napping. The kitchen was quiet enough that the instincts and urges tormenting Ellie couldn't be quieted. To get her mind off her own troubles, she focused on Ava's date.

"So how'd it go?"

"It was fun." She peeked up from the pages she was separating for Ellie's signature. "We're going out again over the weekend."

"Really?" Ellie kept her voice light and found she actually did feel better forgetting about herself and talking about Ava.

Ava's face reddened endearingly. "Mark is a very nice man."

Ellie rolled her eyes. "That's all you can say? That he's nice? You're such a romantic."

"And since when are you an expert on romance?"

Since the night before.

Since she'd been kissed with tenderness and honesty that zapped her fear and made her yearn for things she'd long ago forgotten she wanted.

Since she'd felt sexual heat that hinted at pleasure far beyond what she'd ever experienced.

Since she honest to God wondered if she wasn't falling in love.

The thought nearly suffocated her. In love? Oh, Lord! How could she fall in love with a man she couldn't have?

"You're right. I'm not the one to give romantic advice."

Ava sighed. "Ellie! I was teasing."

"I know, but I'm still not the one to be giving advice."

Ava laughed. "Good grief, girl! You are *Magic*. You are the advice giver." She glanced around the kitchen. "What the heck is happening to you here?"

Ellie pulled in a breath. "I'm losing touch with reality."

"Since when did you deal in reality?"

"Since my intuition went on the fritz."

"I find it hard to believe that your intuition is on the fritz. Why would the woman who's been right on the money with every premonition she's had suddenly decide she had no more intuition?"

"Because I'm always wrong when it comes to myself and men."

"Really?"

"Yes! That's how I know the weird vibes I've been getting here have to be wrong."

"What vibes?"

Ellie debated telling Ava the truth. She was going crazy with sadness one minute and going crazy wishing for things she was sure she couldn't have the next. But the worst were the times when she genuinely believed she could have everything she wanted from this little family, if she'd just say the word. If that was true, and she walked away, let fear control her, then Sam was winning. Ruining her life when he wasn't even around.

Ava was older, wiser, able to discern things. Maybe instead of intuition she needed real advice from someone with experience?

"All right. You asked for it. I'll tell you. My intuition keeps telling me Mac is the man of my dreams. The love of my life."

Ava gaped at her. "No kidding. He's quite a catch. I'd be tempted to take that premonition and run with it."

"This from the woman who hasn't dated in thirty years."

"My situation was different. I was married for twenty years before my husband died. I had known what it was like to be blissfully in love. I'd had children. I'd built a very satisfying life. I already had my good memories. I didn't fear another relationship. I wasn't sure I wanted one." She caught Ellie's hand. "You, on the other hand, are afraid."

"You're damned right I'm afraid."

"Mac is, by all accounts, a wonderful guy. Even you've told me that."

"He is."

"And does he feel the same way about you?"

Ellie whispered, "He kissed me last night."

"Ah." Ava squeezed Ellie's hand. "I don't think there's any reason to be afraid, but if you are, there's a simple cure. Take this slowly. Get to know him. And everything will turn out fine."

"Right."

"You don't sound so sure."

"I have my reasons."

Ava's face fell in concern. "Like what?"

"For one, his ex-wife is a movie star! How could I possibly believe I'm in his league? What if I'm setting myself up for a colossal fall just because my instincts really want for me to belong here?"

"So in other words, you're afraid because your intuition is telling you you belong here and you're questioning it?"

Ellie took a breath. "I've spent my whole life listening to my intuition, and in this house it's seriously on the fritz. I feel lost not being able to trust it."

"Well, if you don't trust your intuition, there's another way to analyze this. Think about what you would listen to if you didn't have intuition."

Ellie frowned. "What else is there?"

"Your head and your heart. What do they say?"

"Well, my head knows that he's a fabulous dad, a good man."

"And your heart?"

"My heart thinks he's wonderful."

"Oh, my dear, Ellie." Ava rose from the kitchen table. "You've already made up your mind. Now you just have to get over your fear, and the best way is what I've already said. Get to know him. Take your time."

"What if he goes faster than I can handle?"

"Then you just pretend he's one of the Happy Maids' employees who won't listen to your instructions."

Ellie laughed. "Are you telling me to fire him?"

"No. I'm telling you to stand your ground."

Ellie rolled her eyes. "Right."

"I am right. That *is* what you need to do. When he gives you work instructions you have to listen. But when the mood turns romantic, you're in charge. If he goes too fast, pull away…walk away." Ava patted Ellie's hand one more time for good measure. "Trust me. You'll know what to do."

"I hope you're right."

"Right about what?"

Both Ava and Ellie spun to face the butler's pantry as Mac walked through into the kitchen.

"I…um…" Ellie stammered, unable to think of anything to say.

Luckily, Ava picked up the ball. "Ellie and I are in charge of a Labor Day picnic for the woman at a charity we work for. I told her we wouldn't have to worry about finding a place even though it's late and everything's already booked."

"That's why I hope she's right," Ellie jumped in, glad for Ava's perfect cover story. "We don't want to have to cancel the picnic just because we were a little slow on the uptake."

Mac set his briefcase on the counter. "How many attendees?"

"Counting workers, we have about thirty."

"This place can accommodate thirty people."

Ava's eyes widened in surprise. Ellie gasped. "You'd let us have a picnic here?"

"Sure. I have a pool, a big yard and a gazebo with a huge grill. I think this place is perfect for a picnic."

Ellie shook her head in dismay. "We can make quite a mess."

"I'll hire Happy Maids to do the clean up the next day."

Ava pulled a pen from her purse and a small notebook. "Sounds good to me. I'll call Ayleen and tell her we can stop looking. We're having our Labor Day picnic here." She smiled at Ellie.

Ellie faced Mac, so flabbergasted by his generosity she was surprised she could speak. "Thanks. You don't know how much we appreciate this."

He waved his hand dismissively. "I think that gazebo was built for parties, yet I've only grilled hot dogs for the kids. It'll be good to see the house get some use."

"True," Ellie agreed, loving the fact that he was coming out of his shell because of her.

"Besides, Lacy will enjoy it."

"Exactly. Plus, we won't be here all day. Most of the guests will arrive around four. We usually clear out around nine or ten," Ava said, obviously not about to let Mac change his mind. She faced Ellie again. "I'll see you tomorrow."

Ellie walked on air the rest of the afternoon as Mac worked in his office. He let her serve dinner and clean up while he played with the kids, and took charge of getting Lacy and Henry ready for bed. He even stepped back when she came into the bedroom to kiss Lacy good-night. Then he said good-night to her and headed for his own room without so much as a hint that he might kiss her.

Relief rippled through her. Then she wondered why. She wanted this. She wanted to be romantically involved with him. She knew Mac was a good man. His light kiss might have been his way of telling her he wouldn't push. And tonight's behavior might have been his way of reinforcing that. So, why was she so worried?

She made her way to her suite, undressed and got into bed. Thoughts of Mac again filled her head. And she did something she hadn't done in years. She discounted her intuition and really thought about him. She thought about his life, his bad marriage, the way he behaved with his kids. She thought about how he'd strong-armed her into taking this job then apologized. She considered how well he treated her and even how he'd changed his mind about letting Ava come to the house as a show of trust.

That was the one that pushed her over the top. He wasn't just fair; he treated her like an equal. Even though she was his employee and he didn't owe her any explanations or apologies, he admitted his mistake in yelling at her, and eventually gave her her own way on the situation, telling her Ava could come to the house to do the daily reports for Happy Maids.

Sam would have never done that.

For a few seconds she also thought about Sam, but they were very important seconds. Not because she once again realized how different Mac was than Sam, but because she realized how different *she* was.

It might have taken her three years to get beyond the emotional hurts enough that she could mature into the person she was supposed to be, but she'd done it. Thanks to Liz. Thanks to A Friend Indeed. She was normal. Finally.

The next morning she awoke feeling totally different. She was a strong, vital woman, who had gotten beyond a bad past. She was different. She was ready.

This time when Mac came into the kitchen and asked for French toast as a way to celebrate Lacy's second day of sleeping until almost seven, she didn't wonder about her place in his home. She didn't burst into tears with fear over losing this little family. She told herself she had choices. She'd take them one at a time and see where they led.

She set the plate of French toast on the table, along with syrup and fresh fruit.

Mac glanced up at her, his blue eyes soft and appreciative. "Thanks."

"You're welcome." She turned to go, but stopped herself and pivoted around again. "You know what? I'm kind of hungry myself."

She took a plate from the stack Mac had brought to the table. She'd thought it was a mistake that he'd brought three plates, but what if it wasn't? What if he wanted her to have breakfast with them?

"I think I'll have some French toast, too."

Lacy said, "All right!" as Ellie sat, snagged two slices of French toast and slathered them with syrup.

"I'm taking the helicopter to Atlanta this morning," Mac said, for the first time ever telling her his plans for the day, really making her feel like part of the family.

Instead of second guessing why he'd done that, instead of panicking over what she "should" say, Ellie simply said the first thing that popped into her head. "That sounds like fun."

"Well, it is and it isn't. I have to attend a meeting of the executive board."

"Who's on your executive board?" Ellie asked, taking Ava's advice that she needed to get to know him. This was his world. The more she knew, the more she'd be able to ascertain if she wanted to be in it.

"My parents retired last year and we replaced them with two cousins." He grinned at her. "You'd be proud of us. One's a woman."

"I'm not that much of a feminist."

"No, but you like to make sure the men in your life aren't chauvinists."

Because it was true, she couldn't deny it. But his observation lightened her heart as much as the third plate had. He was noticing her. Thinking about her. He wasn't going into this mindlessly, either.

After another fifteen minutes of eating and chatting, Mac rose from the table. "Okay. I've got to go now." He kissed Lacy, kissed Henry and faced Ellie, who had risen from the table when he had.

Her heart thundered in her chest. Would he kiss her? First the baby, then the child, then his…girlfriend? Good Lord, she didn't even know how to categorize herself.

But he didn't kiss her. He didn't even make a move to get any closer. He simply smiled. "I'll see you tonight. If all goes well, I won't be late. If I'm not here before six, have dinner with Lacy."

"Okay."

He held her gaze a few seconds longer. He wanted to kiss her, she could see it in his eyes. But he wasn't making any kind of move and she couldn't tell if she was supposed to. And even if he was waiting for some kind of sign from her, what kind of sign would she give him?

She had absolutely no idea. Worse, she'd be mortified
if she guessed wrong. So she stepped away. "If you're late,
Lacy and I will eat without you."

When he left, Ellie collapsed on her chair. Lacy said,
"Are we going to swim before it gets too hot?" bringing
Ellie back to the real world.

But she was grateful to be back. As Ava had said, she
did need time to adjust. Time to get to know him. Time to
adjust to this relationship. And smaller steps were better.

Mac arrived home exhausted. His two cousins were idiots.
They were only on the executive board thanks to the good
will of Mac's parents, yet they had attacked him, attacked
his business practices, attacked his overprotective attitude
with their employees, especially abroad, insinuating that
the money spent on security was wasted.

The money they spent on security was a pittance compared to some of their other expenses. And his cousins'
attacking that small sum only proved how little they knew
about running a business.

He'd called his parents, asked them to remove the cousins, but they'd refused, telling Mac he would have to help
them learn the ropes. They were family and Carmichael
Incorporated was run by family. Because Mac was their
only child, if something happened to him, someone in the
family had to be properly trained to take over.

Fabulous. So now he had months if not years of tolerat-
ing their attitude, while trying to show them the important
things they should be focused on.

He walked through the butler's pantry into the kitchen,
expecting to see Lacy at the table or Ellie bustling around,
only to find the room was empty. He looked at his watch
and groaned. It was nearly ten. Lacy should be sound
asleep. Ellie was probably in her room.

Disappointed, he dropped his briefcase on the table and went in search of leftovers. He found roast beef and mashed potatoes and carrots and took them to the counter. He got a plate so he could divvy out a portion and microwave it, just as Ellie raced into the room.

"I'm sorry! I'll get that," she said, scrambling to the counter and bumping him out of the way.

He bumped her back. "I'm fine."

She tried to take the spoon from his hand. "I know. But this is my job."

Resisting the urge to laugh, he held on to the spoon. "It's nearly ten. Your workday is done."

Looking confused, she said, "Okay," and stepped out of his way, but she didn't leave the room.

Mac's heart rate sped up. Maybe she didn't want to leave the room? That morning she'd had breakfast with them and chatted with him about his day.

Maybe he could entice her into staying while he ate. There was nothing worse than eating dinner alone, but more than that, he enjoyed her company. Plus, it was another step toward them getting to know each other. Another step toward her, hopefully, making a romantic move.

"My cousins turned out to be pains in the butt."

A laugh escaped her. "Really?"

He winced. "Maybe I shouldn't call them pains as much as I should say they don't have any experience."

"So they asked a lot of questions."

He slid his supper into the microwave. "All the wrong questions. Which means that maybe my parents promoted them prematurely."

"Ouch."

He set the timer and shrugged out of his suit jacket and hung it across the back of an available chair before leaning against the countertop. "I asked them to remove them from the board and they asked me to train them."

She casually took a seat at the table. "And what did you say?"

"I said I'd train them."

"That's very nice of you."

The microwave buzzer beeped and he turned to retrieve his dinner. "Not really. It's what my parents want and I always try to please them."

She laughed. "So you're not the family rebel?"

He set his dish down at the place across from her. "No. Just your garden variety family grouch."

She chortled merrily. "You're not a grouch. You just like things done a certain way. Ava tells me Cain is the same way."

He filled his fork with mashed potatoes. "Have you heard from the newlyweds?"

"Ava got a call last week. I think they're ignoring us."

"Wonder why?"

Ellie laughed again and Mac's fork stopped halfway to his mouth. He loved to hear her laugh, but he loved even better that he was the one making her laugh. He shoved the mashed potatoes into his mouth to cover the fact that he was staring at her. When the buttery mixture hit his tongue, he groaned in ecstasy.

"These are fabulous."

"I know! I love them. The secret is tons of butter."

"Whatever the secret, I'm glad you know it."

"Me too."

The conversation died, and silence stretched out. Mac could have thought of a hundred questions to ask, a hundred things to say, but he was hungry. Besides, he wanted her to be a part of this learning process. He wanted her to talk to him, not just answer his questions.

She drew an imaginary line on the table, focusing her attention on that, Mac believed, so she didn't have to look at him when she said, "I missed out on things like family recipes, holiday traditions, so I sort of make up my own."

"Nothing wrong with that."

She glanced up at him. "Really?"

"I think it's a great idea. My family has traditions like going to the Bahamas for Christmas. But I'd rather have an old fashioned Christmas...up north. Maybe in Vermont." He caught her gaze. "Someday I'm going to do that for my kids."

She smiled at him. "That's very nice."

"And a little selfish. I'd like to spend Christmas somewhere that it snows. I want to see snow-covered lights twinkling on Christmas trees."

"I grew up in Wisconsin." She turned her attention to the table again. He wondered if she was debating what to tell him, how much to tell him, and silently begged her to tell him everything.

"I've seen lots of snow."

When she fell silent he decided to nudge her. She'd told him the beginnings of plenty of things, enough that he could question her without her realizing he already knew most of what she would say. "What happened to your parents?"

"I don't know. The story is my mom left me in the vestibule of a church. No one knew who she was. So, obviously, no one knows who my dad is either." She caught his gaze. "Everybody thought I'd be adopted...since I was only about six weeks when I was dropped. But somehow or another I fell through the cracks."

He almost cursed. Her story should have saddened him; instead he was angry. He knew the pain of being abandoned if only because he'd watched Lacy live through it. But Lacy had him and Mrs. Pomeroy. Ellie had had no one. Everybody had let her down.

Again, the intense urge to protect her rose up in him. But he squelched it. She didn't want protecting. She wanted normalcy. And, for them, normalcy was acting on the sexual attraction that pulsed between them. If he really wanted to do the right thing for her, he would create such a wonderful future for her that she'd never again think about the past.

That almost caused him to drop his fork. Already he was thinking about a future with her. He wasn't sure if they were right for each other. But he did know it felt right. He absolutely couldn't say that he loved her. But he did know he was falling.

Still, it all hinged on her and he couldn't rush her. This had to be done on her timetable. Unless she told him she wanted a future with him, he couldn't make assumptions.

He finished his dinner and helped her clear the kitchen. When she turned to go up the stairs, he debated walking with her. He was bone tired and ready for bed, but he didn't want to scare her or push her.

At the same time, he needed to behave normally and he was tired. He should be on his way to bed. Maybe the thing to do would be stop overthinking and simply do what came naturally?

"I'm coming too."

They walked up the stairs together silently. At the top of the steps, instead of opening her door, or even grabbing the knob, Ellie simply stopped.

Mac froze. Was this the sign he kept looking for from her? She'd obviously waited up for him...but she could have waited up to fulfill her responsibility as his maid by warming his dinner. Even her talking to him while he ate could be ascribed to her only wanting to do her job by needing to wait to clean up the kitchen after he was done eating.

Damn. He had forgotten how nerve-racking dating could be.

She pulled in a breath. Mac struggled not to watch her chest rise and fall with it.

"So, I'll see you in the morning."

"Yeah."

She put her hand on the knob, turned it slowly, but still didn't make any move to go inside.

But just when Mac got the courage to take a step toward her, she turned and disappeared behind the door.

Damn it. This was not going to be easy.

"Maybe he doesn't like me?"

Ava laughed. "Just because he didn't kiss you good-night?"

"The mood was set. The time was right. Yet he backed away."

Ava harrumphed as she rose from the table and gathered the papers Ellie had just signed. "He's a wealthy man, potentially falling in love with his maid...plus, he had a fairly crappy marriage. You don't think he has a right to be cautious?"

Ellie grimaced. "I see your point."

"Or maybe he's waiting for you?"

"For me? For me to what?"

"For you to kiss him this time."

"Oh, no. No. No. No. I have to be sure this is what he wants and the only way I know that is if he makes all the moves."

"Well, he's been burned once. So he wouldn't want to enter into a relationship that he wasn't at least reasonably sure of. Plus, you're the help. Technically, you're a sexual harassment suit waiting to happen." She headed for the butler's panty. "You can't just come right out and say, 'I won't sue you if you kiss me,' but I'm guessing you're going to have to give him some kind of sign."

With that Ava opened the garage door. She said, "See you tomorrow," and was gone.

Ellie sat at the table pondering what Ava had said. She'd already realized she'd have to give him some kind of sign. But kiss him? That was too scary for her to contemplate. What would she do? Stand on her tiptoes and just press her lips to his? That would take so long that he'd realize her intention and have time enough to back away if she'd read this whole situation wrong.

Oh, God! That would be so embarrassing!

She wouldn't risk it.

She had to think of a way to get her point across without actually saying or doing anything.

Yeah. Like that would be possible!

Still, she was a creative woman. Surely, she could think of a way to say, "I think I'm falling in love with you" without actually saying those very words.

Perusing the cookbook Ava had given her, she found a recipe for lemon garlic chicken and remembered how much he'd liked the roast beef. He hadn't kissed her after the roast beef, but they had had their most personal conversation as he'd eaten it. So maybe the way to a man's heart really was his stomach?

She cooked the chicken and almost made mashed potatoes, thinking she would go with her strong suit, but in the end decided that would be too obvious.

Of course, she also knew she was going to have to be somewhat obvious or he wouldn't get the message. She found candles and a lace tablecloth for the dining room table, but when she dimmed the lights and lit the candles, the scene was so romantic that she knew it would be weird with Lacy also sitting at the table.

Not exactly the right time for seduction.

She blew out the candles and carried them back into the kitchen so Mac wouldn't see them and wonder why they were on the table but not lit.

He arrived right on time, kissed the kids, changed his clothes and was at the table with Lacy the way he usually was a few minutes after six. Without waiting for an invitation, Ellie sat down at the place she'd set for herself across from Mac at the far end of the long table. They had a pleasant conversation with Lacy, who sat between them on the right.

But the very second Mac finished his chicken, he bounced from his seat, explaining that he had a conference call, and ducked out of helping with clean up.

Which, technically, was his right as boss.

She sighed and instructed Lacy to grab the napkins while she got the dishes. She and Mac's six-year-old daughter cleared the dining room and played Yahtzee while the dishwasher ran.

She got both Lacy and Henry ready for bed with no sign of Mac, then retired to her own room to come up with Plan B.

Unfortunately, she fell asleep before a Plan B could form. So she decided to stick with the one thing she knew consistently got Mac's attention. Food. Once again using a recipe she found in Ava's cookbook, she baked homemade muffins for breakfast. Lacy thought she'd died and gone to heaven. Mac, however, raced into the kitchen, telling Ellie and Lacy that he had another early-morning meeting and was out the door without even as much as a whiff of a muffin.

Disappointed, Ellie dropped to one of the kitchen chairs. The only explanation was that she'd totally misinterpreted everything. Obviously, Mac liked having a casual relationship with her. He wanted her to eat with them. He wanted the kids to be comfortable with her at the table.

But everything else must have been Ellie's imagination.

What about that kiss?

It hadn't been a kiss. It had been a brush. An accident. An accident.

And she had better let it go!

As was their custom, after breakfast, Ellie and Lacy put Henry down for a nap, then they changed into swimsuits and went to the pool. She and Lacy played for an hour then Lacy set up a tea party in the grass for her stuffed animals and dolls while Ellie stretched out on a chaise lounge to enjoy the sun.

Twenty minutes later, the sound of Mac's car roaring up the driveway interrupted their quiet morning. She sat up on the chaise as Lacy rose from her gathering of stuffed animals.

Mac appeared around the side of the house. "Hey, kitten," he said to Lacy.

"Hey, Daddy."

He turned his attention to Ellie. His mouth opened as if he were about to say hello, but his gaze fell to her swimsuit and whatever he was about to say was apparently forgotten.

He wasn't the first man to notice her figure, especially in the royal blue bikini, but he was the man she wanted to notice. And right now he was noticing.

Hope swelled inside her. Maybe the kiss hadn't been an accident?

"I forgot my briefcase."

He said the words, but he didn't make a move to go into the house and get the darned thing. Instead, he stood staring at her.

All right. She didn't need intuition to tell her he was attracted to her. But she'd known that. They'd been attracted since the day they'd met. What she wanted from him was for him to act on that attraction as he'd said he wanted to the night in the gazebo.

Of course, she really couldn't expect him to kiss her in front of his daughter.

She rose from the chaise and slipped into her white lace cover-up. With one hand on Lacy's shoulder, she guided all three of them up the steps.

Needing to get his attention and the conversation back to a safe place for Lacy's sake, she said, "You also left without breakfast."

They reached the French door and Mac opened it, allowing Ellie and Lacy to enter before him.

"I made muffins."

He stopped three steps into the kitchen. "Homemade muffins?"

She laughed. "Don't get too crazy with appreciation. The recipe was really simple."

"Can I take one with me? I really didn't have time for this trip. But I—I—really needed my briefcase."

She frowned, almost asked him why he hadn't sent someone to get his briefcase and suddenly understood.

He'd left so quickly that morning he hadn't had time to interact with either his kids or her. So he'd made an excuse to come home again.

It was the sweetest thing she'd ever seen a man do. Though she wouldn't press him to admit it, she did decide he deserved a reward.

"Sure. I'll wrap one for you while you get your brief-case."

Lacy hooked her arms around Mac's leg, proof that she had been missing him as Mac obviously suspected. He glanced down at her. "Maybe I can take five minutes to eat a muffin." He peeked over at Ellie. "Sit with us while I do?"

"Sure."

She set several muffins on a plate and took it to the table with three dessert dishes. Mac hoisted Lacy to a chair. He took his seat at the head of the table and smiled at Ellie as she took her seat opposite him.

Ellie's world righted again. And suddenly Plan B be-came abundantly clear.

Mac walked down the back stairs after tucking Lacy into bed that night. Ellie had kissed her good-night and scam-pered out of the room fairly quickly, so he wondered if there was something wrong. He wasn't surprised to find a note from her on the table in the kitchen, telling him that she needed to talk with him.

The fact that she asked to meet him in the gazebo was a bit puzzling, but not that she wanted to talk. He'd sensed for days that something was bothering her. He'd waited and waited and waited for a sign from her that she'd been okay with him kissing her. But though she'd eaten meals with him and the kids, other times she'd actually been more distant.

Walking down the stairs and past the pool to the grass, he racked his brain trying to think if he'd said something wrong, or even something too suggestive. But he couldn't think of anything.

Which was why he didn't notice that the gazebo was dark until he reached it. He climbed the two steps into the little room and saw the space was illuminated by only a few thin candles. Ellie stood behind the wet bar. Wearing a long dress made of material so insubstantial it basically floated around her, she walked out from behind the bar and handed him a glass of Scotch.

"Glenfiddich," she said, naming his favorite brand.

"How did you know?"

"The article when you were bachelor of the month is archived on the Single Girl Magazine Web site." She stepped close and smiled at him. "I like to be prepared."

So did he, and tonight he felt at a distinct disadvantage. Not only had she done a little research so she'd know his favorite drink, but also she wore the magnificent flowing dress, created, he was sure, to send a man's temperature into triple digits.

He caught her gaze. Was this the sign he'd been waiting for? "I'm underdressed."

"You're fine."

"You said you wanted to talk?"

"Yes." She turned away and walked to the far side of the gazebo. "You kissed me the other night."

Oh, God. This wasn't a sign. She was leaving. She might be dressed like a temptress, but she was such an innocent about some things she probably didn't realize the dress was seductive. She'd called him here for privacy so she could tell him she was leaving without the kids overhearing. The drink had been to soften the blow.

"And since then we've had a sort of different relationship."

"But not a bad one." He wasn't letting her go without a fight. The kids loved her. His feelings for her were growing with leaps and bounds. His gut was telling him they could have something wonderful. He'd be a fool to just let her quit.

She turned on a bubbly laugh. "I know. I've been very happy these past few days, being a part of things."

"Then why are you leaving?"

"Leaving?" She took a few steps toward him. "I'm not leaving."

"Then why are we here? Why are you softening me up with liquor?"

"Because I'm nervous and I wanted a way to give myself a little time before I told you…" She sucked in a long breath.

Mac stood staring at her, his muscles tight with the tension of anticipation, his breathing barely discernable.

"I trust you."

Another man probably would have wanted to hear something like "because I'm attracted to you." Or "I can't resist you." But Mac knew having Ellie say she trusted him was damned near a declaration of love.

He took two steps toward her. "Really?"

"I know that sounds silly."

He took another two steps, set his drink on the plastic table in the center of the gazebo. "No. You've told me you had a difficult life. But I've had a bad marriage. Trust is very important to both of us."

She took two steps toward him. "I think we want the same things."

"A home. Happy kids." He took another two steps. "Plus, we're attracted."

She laughed. "Yeah. There is that." The final two steps she took put her directly in front of him. His hands slid around her waist as hers slid around his neck.

This time when their lips met there was nothing tentative about the kiss. His mouth slanted against hers with the force of all the pent up sexual frustration he'd been feeling since she walked into his life. Arousal hit him in a dizzying wave of hunger for her. The need was so strong, so intense, he forced himself to pull back a bit, to gentle the press of his mouth on hers. But he wanted her. There was no denying that he wanted her. And, because the need was so strong and so sharp, not for the first time he worried that it was manipulating his common sense. He'd rushed things with Pamela and had been so wrong. Now he was rushing with Ellie. The only way this would work would be if they could take it slow.

Reluctantly, he pulled away completely.

She smiled at him. "Wow."

"Yeah, wow."

"We better watch how many times we do that or we'll get ahead of ourselves."

He rubbed his hand across the back of his neck. "I was just thinking the same thing."

"So we better take things slowly."

He marveled at her. How had he ever found someone this beautiful and this sweet? And this much on his wave length? Did he actually deserve her?

"Okay."

She blew out the first of the three candles and said, "Walk me back to the house?" as she walked to the second and third.

When the gazebo was totally dark, she strolled over to him and he caught her hand. "Sure."

He was absolutely positive he was the happiest man in the world, even with the little voice in the back of his head insisting something was wrong. With both of them in agreement that they should take this slowly, he couldn't see anything wrong with what they were doing. Yet, the little voice kept insisting that he was forgetting something.

Something important.

CHAPTER TEN

MAC didn't exactly stop looking for a nanny, but he didn't feel the pressure to get one immediately. He and Ellie took care of his children, not as a maid and her boss, but more like parents. Each night after they put the kids to bed, they spent romantic evenings in the gazebo or the pool, almost as if they were dating. Then he would kiss her good-night at her bedroom door.

Without any more discussion than the one they'd had in the gazebo, they took everything slowly. Kisses had grown into passionate interludes that didn't go beyond a certain point because he didn't want to rush her. He didn't want to be rushed. And the little voice that insisted there was something important about this relationship dimmed until it was gone.

June quickly became July. Newlyweds Cain and Liz came home. Mac didn't know how Ellie explained her work situation to her boss, but she had to have said something because Ellie continued to work for him and Ava stopped dropping by with Happy Maids sheets to be signed.

After the one trip to the mall, Ellie stopped trying to get Mac to loosen the reins on his security. Mac suspected she hadn't mentioned it again because she enjoyed being in their own little world, alone with only each other for company for the past few weeks while they explored their budding relationship. But one Thursday night in mid-July, Ellie suggested that they invite Cain and Liz for dinner the following night.

At first Mac balked at the idea of bringing strangers into his home when Phil and his crew wouldn't have enough time to investigate them. But with everything going so well for him and Ellie personally, he decided maybe she was right. He didn't want to live in a prison. He didn't want his kids living in a prison and most of all he didn't want to put Ellie in another prison.

That was the "thing he was forgetting" that had been nagging at him about starting a relationship with Ellie. She'd lived in a prison once. He couldn't put her in another. He had to get over his fears, and work himself and his family into the real world. Which meant he couldn't investigate every single person who came into his home. Trusting Ellie's word that Liz and Cain Nestor were good people had to be enough.

So he told her yes, she should invite the Nestors, and the next day he arrived home to a happy Lacy and Henry sitting in the gazebo while Ellie prepared the place for a barbeque.

"You have twenty minutes to get changed into shorts and a T-shirt," she said after placing a smacking kiss on his lips.

"So this dinner is informal?"

"Yes. I didn't want to exclude the kids. Though Ava is coming over at seven to read to them before putting them into bed, I want them to eat with us."

He loved that she thought of his kids. Not as a maid, not even as a nanny, but as someone who loved them. "Ava doesn't mind?"

Ellie laughed merrily. "Are you kidding? She misses the kids now that she doesn't have to come over every day."

The thought that an outsider, someone who didn't have to like his kids, was eager to babysit filled his heart with emotion he couldn't even describe it. Something was happening to him. Something significant. And it was all wrapped up in having Ellie in his life.

The Nestors arrived. Cain in khakis and a golf shirt and pretty brunette Liz in shorts and a T-shirt. Mac recognized Cain from a few casual meetings they'd had at parties and charitable events. Ellie and Liz kept the conversation lively through dinner and after they'd eaten barbequed ribs and scalloped potatoes, Ava arrived and shuttled the kids into the house. After an hour, Ava returned to the gazebo, baby monitor in hand, announcing the kids were both sleeping and Ellie volunteered to walk her to her car.

That was when Mac began to figure everything out. With another couple seated in the comfortable patio chairs in the seating arrangement of the gazebo, his children being cared for by a new friend, and a real relationship developing between him and a wonderful woman, Mac suddenly, unexpectedly, felt normal. He liked being able to trust. Especially Ellie. All this time he'd been working to help Ellie feel normal but he was the one who was changing, being introduced to a totally different way of life.

He glanced around his well-lit, but rather small property. This residence wasn't like the compound he and Pamela had lived in with his parents in Atlanta. This place was a home. Cain and Liz weren't like the stuffy society friends he'd rubbed elbows with his entire life. They were real people. Nice people. And Ellie wasn't anything like the women he typically dated. She was simply a happy, charming woman who enjoyed sharing his life. His life. His *real* life. Not a prison.

Swirling the Scotch in the glass in hand, Mac said, "So, Cain, I understand your company's been courting mine for about ten years."

As Mac expected he would, Cain laughed. "I wouldn't say ten years. Eight maybe."

Carrying the baby monitor, Ellie returned from the driveway.

"No talking business," she said, sitting beside Mac.

He unobtrusively took her hand. "All right. Ellie's right." He glanced at Cain again. "Call me this week."

Cain raised his glass as if in salute and said, "Will do."

Ellie bounced up from her seat. "Cain, it looks like you need another drink." She rounded the bar and lifted the bottle of vodka then frowned. "We're out of ice."

Mac rose. "I'll get it."

Ellie said, "Great," and busied herself behind the bar. She didn't seem to notice that Liz also rose and faced Mac.

"I'll help get the ice."

With his gaze locked with Liz's, Mac easily understood why she'd volunteered. She wanted to have a talk with him. He could have panicked, but his intentions toward Ellie were good. If Ellie's friend wanted to grill him or even just wanted a chance to talk to him privately, he could handle it.

He motioned toward the gazebo entrance. "After you."

They walked up the grassy backyard in silence. Mac suspected that Liz intended to get out of earshot before she said anything. When they reached the pool and she caught his forearm to get his attention, he wasn't surprised.

"Ellie's probably my favorite person in the world."

"Then we instantly agree on something."

"She's sweet and kind and would do anything for anybody."

"I know."

"And I'm going to be very angry if she gets hurt."

Mac laughed, leading her up the steps to the French doors. "I'm not going to hurt her." They reached the top, he opened the door for Liz and followed her inside his kitchen.

"Which means you know about her past?"

Mac pulled an ice bucket from the cabinet. "Bits and pieces."

"Has she told you about Sam?"

He headed for the refrigerator. "Some."

"But not everything?"

"Not yet."

Liz shook her head. "She really is taking this slowly."

Mac caught her gaze. "We both are."

"Okay."

Dumping two handfuls of ice into the bucket, Mac chuckled. "I take it I just got your blessing."

"Not even close. I don't know you. There's so little written about you that I'm not sure anybody knows you."

"Ellie's getting to know me."

"And that's what counts."

He gave her points for speaking her mind and also for being accepting when she didn't hear what she wanted to hear.

"But the thing is Sam really hurt her. She virtually went into hiding for a year after she...she...left him." Liz caught Mac's gaze. "She's too happy, too fun loving, too good with people to be afraid. If you hurt her, I will find you."

"I get it." There was nothing she could do to him, but he understood the sentiment. He loved that Ellie had good friends, strong relationships. It was part of what he wanted with her—part of what he loved about her.

He stopped halfway to the French door. Liz turned around and gave him a puzzled look. "What? Are we forgetting something?"

He rubbed his hand across the back of his neck. "No." He paused, dazed by the realization that he loved Ellie. He *loved* her.

He couldn't. Not that she wasn't wonderful. But he knew better. People who fell in love too fast made mistakes. He wanted to take this slowly. Hell, he'd just told Liz they were both taking it slowly. He *couldn't* love her.

Not yet.

He shook his head a bit to clear the haze then directed Liz toward the French door again. "I'm fine."

Ellie had known the minute she looked at Liz that she was pregnant. She knew it for certain when Liz turned down a glass of wine and asked for a cola with dinner. She hadn't mentioned it in the hope that Liz and Cain would make an announcement. But when they didn't, Ellie had a choice. Wait for Liz to tell her, or simply spill the beans.

The news was too exciting to try to hold back, and she also had to worry that she'd inadvertently let it slip to Ava one day, so she had to out them. When Liz and Mac returned with the bucket of ice, Ellie poured another round of drinks, including a soft drink for Liz.

As she passed the glasses around, she said, "I think I'd like to propose a toast."

Mac laughed. "Really?"

"Yes, to Cain and Liz and their new baby."

Ellie smiled, watching Cain's face fall comically, but Liz only shook her head. "Does anybody ever hide anything from you, Miss Magic?"

Taking her glass of wine to her seat beside Mac, Ellie laughed, but she didn't sit. Mac rose and so did Cain and Liz.

"To your new baby."

"To our baby," Liz and Cain agreed.

"So this is your first child?" Mac asked as they all took their seats.

"Actually, we were married before and had a miscarriage," Liz said quietly.

Before Ellie could come to his rescue, Mac said, "Oh, I'm sorry."

"It's okay," Liz said.

"We had an odd first marriage," Cain said, taking Liz's hand. "My brother died three weeks after we eloped. And for three years after that I was difficult to live with."

"But that's our past," Liz said, smiling at Cain. "And we focus on the future now."

"Having a child is a good way to get yourself in the moment," Mac said.

Knowing a discussion of kids could potentially turn on Mac, and that the last thing he'd want to explain was his situation with his ex-wife and their children, Ellie quickly said, "So, did you ever get the boat you were looking at, Cain?"

Cain launched into a discussion of a new sixty-footer he'd bought right after they returned from Paris, and Mac was more than happy to join in. They shifted from boats to fishing and from fishing to professional football and after an hour Liz yawned.

Cain was on his feet immediately. "You're ready for bed, aren't you?"

"I'm fine."

Understanding Cain's concerns and feeling them herself because of Liz's prior miscarriage, Ellie rose, too. "You're sleepy!"

As Cain pulled Liz to her feet, she yawned again. "I guess I am a bit tired."

"Then we'll say good-night," Cain said to both Ellie and Mac.

Mac said, "We'll walk you to your car."

They strolled up the yard, past the moonlight-dappled pool and to the driveway.

At Cain's car, Mac held out his hand to shake Cain's. "It was nice having you here. Call my direct number on Monday and arrange a lunch with my secretary."

"Thanks, but you know we didn't come here to finagle some business. We wanted to meet the guy who's finally winning Ellie's heart."

Liz slapped Cain's upper arm. "Cain!"

He winced. "Sorry. Was I not supposed to notice that they're living together?"

Liz groaned.

Ellie laughed. "We're not living together, living together. We just happen to live in the same house."

Cain raised his hands defensively. "Sorry. My bad."

The Nestors got into their Porsche. Liz waved goodbye. Cain tooted the horn once and drove out into the starry night.

Ellie stood on the driveway, watching them leave. Before she had a chance to think too much about how seeing Liz reminded her that she was abandoning the life she loved, Mac turned her around, led her into the house and followed her up the steps. When they reached her bedroom door, he walked up behind her, put his arms around her waist and kissed her neck. "We could be living together, living together, if you wanted to."

His smooth lips tickled her neck, but his eagerness to get her into bed tickled her even more. Oh, she was so tempted.

She turned in his arms and he kissed her. This time there was something different in his kiss. This time he didn't start slow and build them to a place where the only thing that existed was each other. This time, his mouth met hers greedily, and, oh, she desperately wanted to simply fall into the kiss. Lose herself in him. Lose herself in the people they were becoming, the life they were creating.

His hands roamed her back, down her bottom and up to her waist again. He seemed restless, hungry, as if only she could fill a void in his life and he was tired of waiting. She kissed him back, letting him know with her kiss that she felt the same way. But in the last second when she would have totally succumbed to the power of need, Mac pulled back.

He stared into her eyes for several seconds then he took a long breath and set her away from him.

"It's still too soon."

She nodded reluctantly. "I think so."

With that she quickly slipped behind her bedroom door. She wanted this so much and so did he that she knew they could very easily make a mistake.

It was better to wait.

Though it got harder and harder to leave Ellie at her bedroom door, the following Monday night Mac counted his blessings as he walked to his suite. It was good to live such a free life. His kids were happy. He was happy. Ellie was happy. They were being cautious, smart. Everything was good.

He wasn't even as concerned about the release of his ex-wife's picture as he had been. The plan was in place. He and the kids weren't at the family compound in Atlanta. They weren't exactly "hiding" but no one really knew where they were. Plus, he had discreet bodyguards and a state-of-the-art security system. He could give Ellie the reasonably normal life she wanted and have a reasonably normal life himself.

That part was perfect.

The only possible hitch was Pamela herself. Tonight she had her first interview scheduled to promote her movie on a late-night talk show. If she focused on her project, Mac, Ellie and the kids would breeze into the next phase of their lives. If she badmouthed him, gave the kids' names or worse held up their pictures on national television, then there would be trouble.

But he couldn't see any reason she'd bring up the kids. She had a movie to promote. Plus, she was trying to get back on track as a Hollywood sex symbol. Kids shouldn't even come up in her conversations.

He entered his suite and slumped into one of the white leather chairs in front of the big-screen TV. He didn't want to have to watch this. Phil had actually volunteered to view the show to see what Pamela would say, but Mac couldn't leave this to Phil. Yes, Phil knew the whole story. But Mac knew Pamela. He could spot one of her lead-ins to trouble a mile away.

He sat through fifteen minutes of monologue and a guest who'd wowed the world with a YouTube video and finally it came time for Pamela.

The host introduced her and she popped from behind a curtain, making her entrance funny. Her long sandy-brown hair swayed around her short sparkly black dress. Mac settled into the chair with a sigh. Ellie ran rings around Pamela any day of the week. He wouldn't deny that his ex-wife was beautiful, but even the way she mugged for the camera so clearly showed that deep down she was an actress, always working the room, always vying for everyone's attention. If she'd ever loved him, it had been only for what he could do for her. He had been a fool for not seeing it.

"So, you have a movie out?" the host said, leading Pam into the discussion that had gotten her onto the very popular show.

"Yes." Her face lit with excitement. "It's a story of a woman who gets involved with a charming man who seems perfect for her. But he's really a serial killer."

Pam again mugged for the camera. Mac rolled his eyes. Phil was right. He didn't need to watch this.

They talked for a few more minutes about the movie. Mac leaned an elbow on the arm of the white leather chair and propped up his head, enduring the inane chitchat.

He was just about to turn off the TV and go to bed when the talk show host said, "I understand you're divorced now."

Mac sat at attention as Pamela's pretty blue eyes drooped with sadness.

"Yes."

"Want to talk about that?"

She pulled in a breath as if considering it, and Mac said a silent prayer that she'd say no. She was on the show to talk about her movie, but Mac knew there was another side to fame. Part of getting people to go to her movies was getting people to like her. He couldn't see how she'd spin their divorce in her favor. The smart thing for her to do would be to simply avoid the topic. Or say something about being back on the market, looking for fun. She was, after all, supposed to be a sex symbol. She shouldn't want to talk about her failure.

He leaned forward, held his breath, said a prayer that she'd simply say no. *Say no. I don't want to talk about my divorce.*

"I loved my husband…"

He slumped back in his chair. *Yeah, right.*

"But sometimes things don't work out."

"Hey, look who you're talking to," the host said, pointing at his chest. "Divorced three times."

Her face fell into sympathetic lines. "Then you know the drill."

"Honey, I invented the drill."

The audience laughed.

Mac breathed a sigh of relief. This really was going okay.

"But I had no kids," the host said, "I understand there was an issue with yours."

Mac's face fell. An issue? What the hell was that supposed to mean?

Pam sat back, laid her hands demurely on her lap and looked for all the world like somebody who didn't want to talk about it. But Mac was familiar with this pose. This was her bid for sympathy pose.

Once again, he leaned forward and prepared himself for the worst.

Pam sighed. "I don't really like to talk about this."

Huh! He was right. She damn well better not want to talk about this. How could she spin giving up her own kids?

"But I don't have the kids." She glanced down at her hands again.

Mac stared at the screen. She was admitting she didn't have the kids?

"I was shocked when my husband took them from me."

What?

Damn her!

Memories of other lies, other deceit came tumbling back, suffocating him. Years of living with her selfishness, years of watching her ignore Lacy, years of feeling like a fool for falling for her so hard, so fast, years of regretting that he'd married her so quickly, all flashed in his head.

He grabbed his cell phone from his jeans pocket, and almost pushed the number for Phil until he realized he had nothing to say. This wasn't a security issue. This was a truth issue. He couldn't do a damned thing about her lie beyond suing her for slander, which would accomplish nothing.

"That is sad," the host said, bringing Mac's attention back to the TV.

"Yes, but I don't want to talk about it."

The host changed the subject and Mac sat back in his chair again, trying to calm himself down, trying to think logically.

All right. So she'd lied. She'd lied before. To him. To his face. At least this time he understood. She'd lied to protect her reputation. It would be foolish to try to do anything about it. Hell, it would be stupid to even get upset. He couldn't expect her to admit she'd walked out on her kids.

He sucked in a breath. He couldn't believe he hadn't seen her for what she was before he married her, but he'd been overwhelmed by her beauty. Almost the way he was being overwhelmed by Ellie's. He stopped his thoughts. There was no comparing Pam and Ellie. None. No way. No how. They were too different.

But *he* wasn't. He was the same guy. Prone to the same mistakes. No matter how slowly he thought he was going with Ellie, as Cain had said, they were living together. Already joining their lives. She'd given up the job she loved. He was letting her into his kids' lives.

What if he was making another mistake?

On a growl, he stopped that train of thought too, turned off the TV and went to his room, focusing on Pam, her deceit. The fallout from this might be a few questions from his friends. His parents might want him to sue her for slander. But he could handle them. His kids were safe. Hell, *he* was safe. She hadn't even used his name.

Life could go on.

And what a good life it might turn out to be.

Ellie liked him. She trusted him.

He trusted her.

The next morning he woke late and raced around to get dressed. Because of a board meeting, he barely had time for a cup of coffee, but when he walked into the kitchen and saw Ellie at the table sitting beside Lacy and feeding Henry, his heart turned over in his chest.

It seemed as if his entire world had righted itself the night before. His ex-wife, though she'd lied, hadn't done the damage she could have done. And the woman he was coming to adore was in his kitchen, smiling at him.

"Good morning."

Her voice was soft, sexy, and everything inside of Mac responded. He never thought he'd see the day when he'd really be free. It wasn't so much the worry of Pam and what she might do, but his own internal fears that had kept him trapped, but Ellie had opened the doors of his heart. She made him feel young, rational, handsome and worthy of love. After the number Pamela had done on him, he almost couldn't believe it.

He walked over to the table and bent down and kissed her. On the mouth, in front of the kids. Lacy giggled. But Mac's heart rate tripled, his pulse scrambled and everything inside him turned to gold.

When he pulled away, Ellie smiled up at him. "Now, that's a good morning."

Lacy laughed in earnest. "Daddy's Ellie's prince."

He held her gaze. He hoped he was her prince. Though she liked him and he liked her, there was so much they hadn't talked about. So much to get to know about each other.

But instead of being afraid, he was excited. Getting to know her would be wonderful.

He pulled away at the same time that his cell phone rang and the roar of cars bounding up his driveway filled the kitchen. He glanced at Ellie, whose eyes had gone round with confusion.

He grabbed his cell phone, saw it was Phil. "What's up?"

"Is everyone in the house?"

"We're all in the kitchen."

"Stay there. We're coming in."

"What's going on?"

"Just stay there. I'm two steps away from the garage."

Phil burst into the butler's pantry and was in the kitchen in seconds. He adjusted a microphone at his mouth. "All clear in the kitchen."

"Did we have a threat?"

Phil held up a hand as he apparently listened to someone speaking through the headset.

Lacy grabbed Mac's leg. Henry began to cry. Ellie jumped up and lifted him from the highchair.

Phil blew his breath out on a sigh. "I got the all clear from the guys outside, but you're all going to have to come outside while they search the rest of the house. Then I'm afraid you're going to have to leave."

Mac's face turned to stone. "Leave?"

"You got an e-mail threat this morning."

"What kind of threat?"

Phil glanced at Ellie and the kids just as one of Phil's top guys, Tom Zunich, stepped into the kitchen. "How about if we talk after Tom takes Ellie and the kids outside to one of our vans?"

Mac turned to Ellie. He knew Phil wouldn't ask him to leave the house if the threat to his life wasn't viable. He was keeping fury and terror at bay by only the barest thread. He needed to talk to Phil to sort this out and Phil was right: he didn't want Ellie and the kids to hear.

"Can you go with Tom?"

She didn't even hesitate. Holding his gaze, letting him know that the words of trust she'd spoken still held, she said, "Sure." She tugged Lacy's hand off Mac's leg. "Come on, sweetie."

Phil and Mac followed Tom and Ellie out of the house. But Tom led Ellie and the kids to a van, while Phil and Mac walked toward the grass.

The second Ellie and the kids were out of earshot, Mac spun on Phil. "What the hell is going on?"

"Did you watch your ex on TV last night?"

"Yes. She lied about the kids, but other than that I didn't hear anything worth worrying about."

"Her lie might have seemed small to you but one of her crazed fans doesn't like the fact that you took her children from her. The e-mail to your private account was very explicit. There will be a bomb. We don't know if it'll be in your house, your car or at Carmichael Incorporated headquarters, but she was serious."

Mac stifled a groan. "Pam didn't even mention my name. How the hell did somebody get to me so quickly?"

"It was common knowledge that your ex was married to you during the time she wasn't making movies. We don't know that the e-mailer found *this* house, but your corporate headquarters and family home are well-known. Plus, the skill level of this person is a variable. A really good hacker can find all of your family's properties."

"But Pam *lied*. She only said that I took the kids to protect her image."

"Yeah, well, she protected it so well that lots of people are standing up for her. You're a hot topic on Twitter. Her Facebook page has gone down twice from too many hits. Her fans are on her side. She was America's sweetheart and you took her kids."

He rubbed his hand across his forehead.

"And one of them was crazy enough to take action." Phil caught Mac's arm, making sure he had his undivided attention. "As a precaution, you can't take any of your cars. You can't go to any of your homes. You're going to have to check into a hotel until our bomb squad can sweep everything." He pulled his BlackBerry out of his jacket pocket. "I've taken the liberty of booking the penthouse suite for you at a hotel in Miami."

Mac smiled ruefully. "You're not going to tell me the name of the hotel?"

"Not until we get there."

The penthouse suite turned out to be the most beautiful place Ellie had ever seen. Green club chairs sat in front of a fireplace with a mahogany mantle trimmed in gold.

Gold and burgundy accent pillows dotted a sofa beside the chairs. An armoire hid a flat-screen TV. A mahogany dining room table was set up just beyond the seating arrangement. A kitchen sat behind that.

Gold trimmed mahogany doors led to three bedrooms. Heavy burgundy drapes on the wall of windows in the main seating area were open to reveal a breathtaking view of the ocean and a tropical storm that was moving in. The waves roared below them, reminding Ellie of Mac's mood.

After they put the children down for a nap, she sat beside him on the sofa.

She took his hand and said, "This too shall pass."

He snorted a laugh, bounced from the sofa and paced to the window. "Really?"

"I have some experience dealing with really bad exes."

He turned and faced her. "Don't tell me…from the A Friend Indeed people."

"And my own experience."

That seemed to stop him cold. He said nothing, merely waited.

She blew out a breath. "I lived with a guy named Sam who seemed like the most wonderful guy in the world until about three weeks after I moved in with him."

Mac took two steps toward the sofa. "Then?"

"Then he became verbally abusive." She shrugged. "At first I blamed it on bad days. Everybody has them. He was a small-business owner." She glanced up at Mac. "He owned four pizza places and sometimes they struggled. Plus, he wasn't as bad as one of the foster parents I'd had. So I figured I could deal with it."

Talking about it resurrected the fear she'd lived for three long years. It crawled along her spine like a living thing. She sucked in a deep breath, blew it out slowly.

"I was a homeless clerk in one of his shops. I didn't have any money. So when we began living together, I didn't bring anything to the table for him. Technically, I was another expense. He lived and died by the sales in each shop every week. His financial future was always on the line."

Mac dropped to one of the club chairs, put his elbow on the arm and his chin on his fist. His own troubles seemingly forgotten, he caught her gaze. "That's one of the risks of owning your own business."

"I know that now. But back then I was eighteen. I saw him as a knight in shining armor, facing battles every day that provided me with a home." She squeezed her eyes shut. "I believed a little too much in fairy tales."

"You were still a kid."

She met his gaze. "I was never a kid."

He shook his head sadly. "I know."

"Anyway, one day about twenty minutes before he should have come home from work, I had this really strong sense that I should toss all my clothes into a suitcase and run."

"The intuition that makes you Magic?"

She smiled ruefully. "Except I didn't run. I couldn't imagine why suddenly that day the intuition that kept telling me to stay, that he was providing me with a place that kept me warm and dry and I needed him, was now telling me to go. I thought I was just being weird."

She swallowed hard and suddenly felt as if she couldn't finish. Fear roamed through her, taking up residence in her stuttering heart, as memories tripped over themselves in her brain.

Mac quietly said, "So what happened?"

"He came home with a gun."

Mac sat up. "What?"

"He came home with a gun. Before I could run he caught my wrist and wouldn't let me go. He yanked me close and put the gun to my head and told me he was going to kill me then kill himself." She shook her head. "He was so out of it, talking about killing us in this romantic way that scared me so much I started to cry."

"My God."

"Crying saved me. It annoyed him and he shoved me away from him. He raised the gun and pointed it at me and I turned and ran. The first shot missed me. The second shot hit the door as it closed behind me." She peeked at Mac. "The rest is sort of a blur."

"I'm sorry."

"Yeah. I was sorry too. Sorry I didn't recognize the signs. Sorry I didn't try to get help...for both of us."

"It wasn't your fault."

She knew that. And, actually, telling Mac the story seemed to allow that truth to penetrate. It was as if telling him had resurrected the ghosts that haunted her, deconstructed them and took away their power to hurt her. She felt distanced from the story. She knew it had happened to her, but it didn't define her anymore. In fact, she felt so beyond that part of her life that she knew she had to tell him the rest.

"The worst part is when it's over. Wondering where he is, what he's doing... Whether or not he's going to find you."

Mac's fury with his ex-wife morphed into fury with Ellie's ex boyfriend. Now he understood why Liz Nestor had wanted to talk with him privately, why she wanted to be sure Mac wouldn't hurt Ellie. She'd been hurt enough already.

"Tell me more about what came after."

"About running and hiding? Living with Liz, fearing that I was dragging her into my mess? Only being able to clean houses of people who were out of town because I was so afraid I'd run into someone who remembered me from a pizza shop." She combed her fingers through her hair and rose from the sofa, walked to the wall of windows. "I was a mess."

"How long did it last?"

"Almost a year, then Liz talked me into coming on one of her assignments for A Friend Indeed. Sharing stories with the other women really helped me snap out of a lot of it." She stared out at the storm. Foamy white waves hit the shore. "But I still wouldn't risk running into anyone in any of the houses I cleaned." She faced Mac with a sad smile. "Liz was very patient."

"Liz is a good friend."

"I know."

"So it's really only been a little over a year or so that you've been out in the world?"

"Almost two." She caught his gaze. "I'm not proud of that."

"You shouldn't be ashamed either." Mac thought of himself, about how hard it had been to get over his anger with Pamela, and realized it had probably been a hundred times harder for Ellie to get over her past. Yet, here he was, dragging her into another relationship. Maybe one even more dangerous.

"You had a right to take all the time you needed to heal."

The penthouse elevator bell rang and the sound of footsteps on the marble foyer floor echoed into the living room. Mac tensed until Phil stepped into the room. "We're getting all clear messages from all of your properties. But I still don't feel comfortable with you going home."

"We're fine here until you say the word."

"And I also think it's time to discuss your new casual attitude," Phil added, glancing meaningfully at Ellie.

She blanched. "I wouldn't ever ask him to do something foolish! To take a risk with his kids!"

"No, but you don't seem to get it. The people who pursue people like Mac are nuts. They can conjure a vendetta out of a simple slight. Real or imagined."

"That's enough, Phil."

"I'm just saying—"

"We get it," Mac said, dismissing him.

With a shake of his head, Phil turned back to the foyer. Within seconds the sound of the elevator bell rippled through the room.

Mac turned to Ellie. "He's right, you know."

"Not always."

"No, but there is no foolproof way to tell when a threat is viable unless you investigate it and that means you can't go to the mall, pretending nothing's wrong. We get threats regularly. Just because of who we are. Now my wife's fans are adding trouble to the mix. Plus, there's all our foreign dealings. We're a target simply because we're global."

Ellie swallowed. "I understand."

He squeezed his eyes shut. "No. I don't think you do." His eyes popped open and he walked over to the wall of windows where she stood. The sea raged. Lightning lit the dark sky. Thunder rattled the windows. "This is my life."

He once again remembered the "something important" that had been nagging at him after the night she kissed him in the gazebo, the night he'd believed if they took this slowly they could make it work. His life was a prison and Ellie deserved better.

"I know."

With one finger on her chin, he tipped her face up until she met his eyes. "I can't change it."

With their gazes locked, she studied him for several seconds, but ultimately her eyes softened. "Okay."

"No, it's not okay." He shook his head. "You think you understand, but until you've lived it you can't understand and it's not right for me to ask you to live this way."

She stepped back. "What?"

"Ellie, you yourself just told me that you've only recently recovered from a really bad experience. My life is a potential smorgasbord of bad experiences. I won't put you through this. I won't steal your life again."

This time the fear that rose up in her was fresh, not remembered. She *loved* him. She knew the risks. She'd rather face them than spend the rest of her life without the one person she genuinely believed loved and understood her.

"I'm not a hothouse flower!"

"I never said you were. You're one of the strongest, smartest women I know. You're also the kindest. It would be selfish and wrong for me to keep you." He sucked in a breath, pulled his cell phone from his pocket and buzzed Phil.

"You may take Ms. Swanson to the Happy Maids' office. Put her into Liz Nestor's hands. Check out the situation to be sure it's safe and assign a bodyguard to her until this threat has passed."

Then he turned and left Ellie alone in the room to wait for Phil because he wasn't sure he was strong enough not to change his mind and beg her to stay.

CHAPTER ELEVEN

MAC and his children stayed at the hotel for an entire week. Mrs. Pomeroy was waiting at his house when they returned. She spent the night, but she wasn't a real nanny and Mac knew his time for procrastination had run out.

The next morning he strode off the elevator into his secluded office, carrying Henry in a baby carrier. Phil marched behind him, carrying Lacy.

"Ashley!"

His personal secretary appeared at the door. Five-nine, reed thin, with auburn hair and an ever present yellow pencil behind her ear, Ashley was a recent university graduate. "Yes, Mr. Carmichael—" She saw Lacy and Henry. "Oh."

"Has Mrs. Davis scheduled those nanny interviews today?"

Mac asked the question as the elevator opened on two of Phil's men. Wearing a dark suit, sunglasses and an ear bud communication device in his ear, Tom carried a playpen and Henry's diaper bag. Similarly dressed, Paul toted a bag of Lacy's toys.

Ashley watched as they set Mac's kids' things in the corner by his desk. Then she faced Mac with a smile. "You're going to have the nannies interact with the children."

He hadn't thought of that, but since they were here that was as good of an excuse as any for having his kids with him. "Yes. Are they scheduled?"

She glanced down at the calendar she held. "One for nine. One at ten-thirty. One at twelve." She closed the book. "Mrs. Davis gave you an hour and a half with each candidate."

Without removing his sunglasses, Tom quietly set up the playpen.

Lacy squirmed until Phil set her down on the floor. "Daddy, I want my doll."

He looked at Tom. "Doll?"

"In the car." He headed for the elevator. "I'm on my way."

Paul followed him. "We should have all the children's things up here in three or four trips, sir."

"That's fine."

Phil headed for the elevator too. "I'll help."

"Great." Mac looked at Ashley. "Have Mrs. Davis send the first candidate in when she arrives."

Ashley's cheeks turned pink. "It's a man."

"Great." Resisting the urge to squeeze his eyes shut, Mac instead reached for Lacy. After all, it didn't matter if it was a man or woman who cared for his kids as long as the candidate was competent.

Ashley raced out of the room. Mac lifted Lacy into his arms. "Tom will set up a place for you to play. You have to be quiet while daddy talks to nannies."

"I want Ellie."

Right.

He understood Lacy's feelings. He wanted Ellie too. Not because she was good with the kids, but because he missed her. He missed being normal. He missed having a real life. He missed having someone to talk to, someone who was interested in him as a person, not because he was rich. Someone who loved him.

Yeah, he wanted Ellie too. But he wasn't so selfish that he'd drag her into this life.

He walked Lacy to the small conference table in the back corner of his office. "I think this would be a great place for you to play."

"What about Henry?"

"He'll nap in the playpen."

As Mac said the last, Mrs. Davis, Mac's longtime administrative assistant, stepped into the room. Dressed impeccably in a navy blue suit, she led a short balding man into Mac's office. "This is James Collins."

Mac offered his hand for shaking. "Mr. Collins."

"Mr. Carmichael. I've heard so much about you."

Undoubtedly. Somehow or another the bomb threat had been leaked. Pamela played horrified actress, using the threat to get her face all over the papers. Mac had had no choice but to let her visit the kids, but he'd set the time and the place and his team had kept the press out. Her crazed fan had been arrested. And now life was going on.

Sort of. Without Ellie it was all kind of gray and lifeless.

Mac pointed toward his desk, indicating he and Collins should talk there. "You've heard so much about us, yet you still want to work for us?"

"Absolutely. In fact, I think I might be your best candidate. I've been in the Marines."

Mac took his seat behind the desk as Jim Collins sat on one of the chairs in front of the desk.

"You should know the children were madly in love with our last nanny."

"Can I ask why she left?"

He wanted to say no. He wanted to say he was afraid for her life, afraid that he'd ruin her life, afraid that he'd stifle her and she'd run...and hurt him a hundred times more than Pamela had. Instead, he glanced down at the résumé Mrs. Davis had surreptitiously set on his desk and said, "Personal reasons."

Ellie unlocked the door of the Happy Maids office and simply stood on the threshold for a good five minutes. Even though it had been a week, she couldn't believe she was here. It seemed surreal. At the oddest times memories would sneak up on her and stop her cold. A little over a week ago, she had been falling in love, mothering two wonderful children. Today she was alone again. Unwanted.

No, she thought, walking to the desk and tossing her purse into the bottom drawer on the right. Mac wanted her. He simply didn't trust her to be able to handle his life.

Tears filled her eyes and she cursed herself. Why was she crying? Hadn't she cried enough? Hadn't she learned a million times over that crying didn't help anything?

She sucked in a breath and stemmed her tears. She had learned that lesson. And she'd also learned that life went on.

She sat at the desk, confused about where to start, what to do. Oh, she loved this job, but it didn't feel like hers anymore. She almost called Ava then couldn't bring herself to do it. How would she explain? What would she say? Liz was home, working a very light schedule, dependent upon Ellie to keep things going, and by God she would.

She was stronger than anybody believed she was. She got over her fear when she left Sam. She'd get over the unbearable sadness of losing Mac.

Hopefully.

* * *

Jim Collins was a great guy and would probably make an outstanding nanny. He also came with the benefit of training in the security field. He'd been trained to handle kids in all the worst-case scenarios Mac envisioned. But the kids hadn't warmed to him. Oh, they liked him enough. Mac liked him. But something was missing.

Mac chalked it up to the fact that Jim was a professional bodyguard. And neither Mac nor his children could see past that. It was almost as if hiring Jim would be like saying they expected more trouble. Mac *did* anticipate trouble. But he also had Phil and his various teams. His hiring a nanny who was also a bodyguard would have driven Ellie crazy.

He told himself not to think about Ellie, to stop filtering his decisions through the question of what she'd do. Not only did he need to get over her, but also she had never once tried to contact him. Even Liz Nestor hadn't made good on her threat to "find" him if he hurt Ellie. So his only logical guess was Ellie was fine without him.

He thanked Jim for coming in and told him that they would get back to him.

The second interview went only slightly better than the first. Mrs. Regina Olson was a widow. She adored children, had raised three of her own, and needed the income. Only in her forties she expected to work until she was sixty-five and would have been blessedly pleased if she could work for the same family that entire time. Especially a family with two gorgeous children.

Unfortunately, she tweaked Lacy's cheeks and Lacy howled in pain. Mac knew Regina hadn't hurt Lacy, but Lacy had not appreciated the tweak. Panicked, Mrs. Olson insisted she hadn't tweaked that hard, but Lacy only cried all the more.

Ms. Nancy Turner was a tall blonde around Ellie's age. Lacy approached her carefully and stood by her chair while Mac tried to ask questions without calling attention to the fact that his six-year-old daughter was staring at her.

Finally, Mac said, "Lacy, come sit on Daddy's lap."

She walked around the desk slowly, backward, not taking her eyes off Nancy Turner.

"So you've been a nanny before?"

"I worked in New York City." She laughed lightly. "Last winter I decided I hated snow. *Really* hated snow," she emphasized, laughing again. "And here I am." She reached into her purse. "Mrs. Davis has my references, but here they are again."

She handed him a sheet with the names of two prominent Wall Street investors, both of whom were personal friends of Mac's. He could see why she'd wanted him to take special note of that.

"That's very good."

"Are you Ellie's sister?"

Nancy smiled at Lacy. "I don't have any sisters." Then she glanced at Mac. "Who is Ellie?"

"Ellie was our last nanny. You sort of look like her."

"I see."

"The children were quite fond of her."

"Of course." She gave Lacy a soft smile. "You can tell me all the things you liked about Ellie, all the things you liked to do with her and I'm sure we can do a lot of those things."

He tried to picture Nancy Turner with a sheet wrapped around her for a make-believe ball gown and couldn't. She looked enough like Ellie that she really could have been her sister. She also had a pleasant disposition, great references and seemed to genuinely like Lacy.

But there was something off. Something wrong.

Nancy unexpectedly rose. She extended her hand to shake Mac's. "I'm sorry, but I scheduled another interview for immediately after this one." She smiled engagingly. "Have to keep all my options open, you know."

Hoisting Lacy with him, Mac rose too. "Of course." He shifted Lacy to sit on his hip. "We'll call you when we've made a decision."

She smiled. "Thank you."

With that she turned and left. Lacy looked up at him and said, "What are options?"

"She wants to make sure she gets a job, so we're not the only people she's talking to."

Lacy simply said, "Oh," then scooted down and returned to the play area Phil had set up in the corner of his office.

Mac buzzed Mrs. Davis. She stepped into the room a few minutes later. "Hello, Lacy."

Lacy said, "Hello, Mrs. Davis."

Pride rose up in him at not just how polite Lacy was, but more than that how she was no longer shy, and Mac instantly remembered that he owed Ellie for that.

She'd told Lacy fairy tales, taught her to shop, told her the value of being good.

And he suddenly knew why none of the nannies had seemed right. None of them was Ellie.

But that was wrong. She didn't belong with them. She had a life. Mac had given it back to her. And she'd never tried to contact him. Not even through her friends. She hadn't really loved him. Didn't want him.

If it killed him to live without her, and it just might, he would.

Even if the next weeks were the hardest of his life, he would push through them.

* * *

The first Monday in September, Mac was at the end of his rope. Lacy was back to waking at four, but now she also refused breakfast. For some reason or another, today, she also didn't want lunch. At four, even knowing dinner wasn't until six, she refused a snack.

Mac had hired a fifty-something grandmother named Blanche to be the nanny. Though she wasn't Ellie, she was more than qualified to care for his kids. As Mac's phone rang, she stooped beside the table tempting Lacy with crackers.

"Please. We'll put cheese on them."

Mac extracted his ringing phone from his jean's pocket and barked, "Yes?"

"Mac?"

Hearing Phil's voice, Mac squeezed his eyes shut. He'd barked at the one person who consistently supported him. He had to get over losing Ellie or he'd alienate everybody in his world. "Sorry. What's up?"

"There's a van here. Woman inside says you told her she could have a picnic here with thirty of her friends. ID says she's Ava Munroe."

Mac's eyes popped open. "Oh, my gosh. What day is it?"

"Monday…Labor Day."

He groaned. "That's the A Friend Indeed group. I did tell them they could have a picnic here."

"Actually, I'm looking at the files in my laptop. You had me check them out a few months ago. And they all cleared. Every person on the guest list."

"And we haven't changed the list."

Mac heard Ava's unmistakable voice coming from somewhere near Phil and sucked in a breath.

"The only people I brought were those you cleared."

Every memory he had of Ava also included Ellie, and pain ricocheted through him. Weeks had passed and he was no closer to getting over her than he had been the day he asked her to leave.

Worse, today, the bomb threat that caused Mac to enact the protocols and procedures to keep him and his children safe seemed so far away. And nothing, absolutely nothing even slightly dangerous had happened in weeks. He and the kids were back to living in a prison and with thirty happy people sitting at his gate, thirty people about to have a picnic, oodles of kids who could potentially make his daughter happy, that prison suddenly seemed oh so unnecessary.

Still, he'd lost Ellie because of the danger in his world. Because he had to erect barriers. Because he couldn't be too careful. If he changed his mind now, if he loosened his restrictions, losing her would be for nothing.

"Tell Ava that I'm sorry. My staff should have called her and told her that with the new security procedures—"

"Give me that phone!"

Mac heard Ava's voice again. Two seconds later her voice, not Phil's, came through his cell phone. "Mac?"

"Hello, Ava."

"You cannot tell a woman with a vanload of kids that she can't use your pool. You promised."

"I know, but—"

"No buts! You *promised*. Besides, I miss your kids." Her voice softened. "Please? I'd love to see Lacy and Henry."

His gaze slid over to Lacy. She sat with her elbows on the table, her lips turned down in a frown, her eyes clouded in misery.

"I heard your guy say that he checked us out," Ava said, sounding angry now. "And there are six guards here. If you're really that afraid of us, leave while we're here and lock your house. All we need is your pool and gazebo anyway."

Realizing how ridiculous he seemed, Mac sighed. He did have six guards. And this was a charity. And it was Ava he was talking with, not Ellie.

He swallowed, wondering why he'd harbored the hope that she'd come. That he'd get to see her. At least he didn't have to worry that he'd see her and melt into a puddle of need at her feet.

"Okay."

Snapping his phone closed, he turned to see Blanche smiling at him. "Okay, what?"

"A friend works for a charity. I promised her that she and some of the kids from the charity could swim in the pool."

Lacy's eyes widened. "Ellie?"

"No, Ellie isn't coming, but Ava is."

Lacy's pretty face fell again. "Oh."

"Hey," Mac said, walking over to her. "You get to swim with some kids. They're going to barbecue. Ava specifically asked to see you."

Lacy nodded. Mac sucked in a breath. He knew exactly what Lacy was feeling but worse. She might adore Ellie, but Mac had loved her. He'd had the promise of a whole new life with her and he'd had to walk away from it.

The sound of cars pulling up the driveway filled the kitchen. The garage door opened and Phil walked up the butler's pantry. They exchanged a look and Mac turned to Blanche. "Why don't you take the kids upstairs? Lacy can get into her swimsuit."

When Blanche and the kids were gone, Phil said, "Seriously, Mac, they're fine. As Ava pointed out I have six guards. We'll be discreet. The kids will have a good time."

Mac said, "Okay," then dismissed Phil. He didn't really want to be a bad host, but, then again, he wasn't really the host of this party. A Friend Indeed was. He could disappear and let Blanche stay with Lacy at the pool.

Lacy came skipping into the kitchen with Blanche on her heels. She was happy because she was finally going to see people other than him and Henry. How could he not let her enjoy this?

He stooped to her height. "All set to have some fun?"

"Yes."

"I'm not going to swim, but I'll watch from the sidelines."

Lacy nodded eagerly and Mac rose and led them to the French doors.

They walked outside to a yard full of people. As Ava introduced Mac to a string of adults who carried coolers and bags of groceries past them to his gazebo, Lacy jumped into the pool with the kids who must have gone straight from the van to the water.

Their noisy laughter filled the air and something inside of Mac shifted, relaxed. He loved that his property was getting some real use. Loved that Lacy was finally smiling. He could handle this.

Then he saw Ellie.

Dressed in white shorts and a pink T-shirt, with her long blond hair floating around her, and wearing big black sunglasses, she made her way from the driveway, carrying a green cooler. She looked soft, happy, so touchable, so kissable.

When she reached him, she stopped. "Hey."

Desire stuttered through him. He couldn't see her eyes, but the smile she gave him was genuine and something tripped in his heart. He wanted to swing her into his arms and welcome her home, but he couldn't do that. He might have relaxed his regulations enough to keep a promise and let a charity hold a party on his grounds. But his life was a trap. A prison. She deserved better.

"Hey."

"So how have you been?"

Miserable. Sad. Lonely. Desperate for you.

"Okay."

"Me too."

She shuffled the cooler she was holding and Mac immediately took it from her hands. "Let me take that to the gazebo."

He expected her to argue, remembered the day she arrived when she'd told him she wanted to carry her own suitcase, but he wouldn't let her. Even then he'd known she was special.

They started walking toward the gazebo. "How are the kids doing?"

"Better."

She pulled the sunglasses down her nose and peeked over the top at him. "They were bad at some point?"

"They don't like the new situation."

"Really? I'm shocked."

He stopped. "Don't. Don't make fun of what I think I have to do."

"Is that what you think I'm doing?" She shook her head. "Don't be ridiculous. I know you need a certain amount of protection. The protection isn't the issue. It's how you handle it that is. You've got bodyguards. Big deal. Lots of people do. You have a fence. So what? Most people do. I'll bet you have alarms and cameras too. Again, what does it matter? A person can't go into a convenience store these days or stop at an ATM without getting his picture taken." She met his gaze. "Precautions aren't the issue. It's accepting them. And being realistic."

Her answer unexpectedly angered him and when she would have turned and walked away, he dropped the cooler and caught her arm. "And you're the expert?"

But rather than be angry that he'd confronted her, she smiled her brilliant smile again and Mac's heart melted. "I am. I had to learn how to stop being overprotective. How to live." She met his gaze with a world of love shining out of her eyes. "If you'd let me, I'd help you."

He swallowed. Everything inside of him screamed that he should take her help. Instead, he stood frozen. Torn between what was good for her and what was good for him.

She picked up the cooler. "In fact, I think you know that I could help you navigate this part of your life. I think the truth is you ran scared. Your ex-wife did such a number on you that you're afraid to try again. I think seeing her on TV reminded you of that, and the bomb scare gave you a legitimate excuse to push me away."

With that she walked away, disappearing into the gazebo, and though Mac wanted to sputter protests that she was wrong—he *was* protecting her from his life, not afraid—he glanced around, actually considering what she'd said. He had bodyguards. But they were discreet. His yard was fenced in. There were alarms and cameras everywhere. But, again, a person couldn't go to an ATM without getting his face on a camera.

Dear God. Was she right? Had he panicked not because of the bomb scare but because seeing Pamela scared him?

Was he punishing Ellie for sins Pamela had committed?

Ellie watched Mac walk away, back to the house, and her spirit deflated. She hadn't intended to harbor the hope that when he saw her he'd realize what he'd lost—what they'd lost—and change his mind.

But she had.

When that hope hadn't materialized, she'd tried shaming him into admitting he'd made a mistake. She'd prayed that his pride would bluster to the surface, and as he argued that he wasn't running scared he'd admit he loved her and wanted her back before his common sense could kick in.

That hadn't happened either.

Now he was leaving. He opened the French doors and in a few seconds was gone from sight. Ellie stared at the door.

She couldn't believe he'd forgotten everything they had. Yet, no matter how strong their feelings, they weren't strong enough for him to take a risk with her.

"Ms. Swanson?"

Ellie glanced to the right to see Phil standing at attention in front of her, wire in his ear, sunglasses reflecting her surprised expression back at her.

He caught her arm. "Would you come with me please?"

"He's kicking me off his property?" Ellie sputtered, remembering how Phil guided her out of the hotel.

Phil said nothing, simply directed her up the steps to the kitchen and from the kitchen back to a hall and from the hall up a set of stairs.

"Everybody at that party saw you take me," Ellie said. "In a few minutes everybody's going to wonder where I am—"

"Then let me suggest you hurry so you can get back out before they do."

Ellie whipped her head around to see Mac following them. "Why? What do you want?"

Mac laughed. "A little privacy."

As if he'd just heard a secret word or code, Phil dropped her arm and walked away. Mac opened the door to an office and motioned her inside.

"After you."

Her heart stuttered then leaped into overdrive. Privacy could mean that he'd thought about what she'd said and agreed with her and didn't want to kiss her in front of thirty strangers. Still, she wouldn't let herself get her hopes up. Not only had he passed on two really good opportunities to tell her he was sorry out by the pool, but his methods for getting her into his house were a bit high-handed.

"You can't keep me here."

"That's been my point all along with us." He sucked in a breath, closing the door behind them. "I wanted to keep you here." He rubbed his hand along the back of his neck. "Hell, I did a great job of actually keeping you here for over two months."

Her eyes narrowed. "What are you saying?"

"I'm saying that you're right. I panicked."

He looked too calm, too normal, to be accepting what she'd said. "Panicked?"

"As long as we were playing boss and maid, I sort of had you locked in."

She frowned. "You let me leave anytime I wanted to. How did you have me locked in?"

"Because I knew you'd come back." He sighed heavily. "But when we really got serious and my life sort of imploded, I realized I loved you and there was absolutely no reason for you to stay."

She gaped at him. "You think I had more reason to stay as a maid than a woman who loved you?"

"So I asked you to leave before you could leave me."

"You are a silly man."

Suddenly Mac's face changed. His expression shifted. His eyes narrowed. "Did you just say you loved me?"

"Of course, I did."

"But you hardly had time to know me. I have a crazy ex-wife, two kids who need a mother, a house that will probably be perpetually surrounded by bodyguards."

"Which makes you really lucky that you found someone who can handle it."

He rubbed his hand along the back of his neck. "Are you sure you know what you're getting yourself into?"

She shook her head. "You have really got to work on your romantic lines. Right about now, you should be saying, 'I love you too' and sweeping me off my feet."

He quietly said, "I love you too." Then he smiled. "I really love you. I really missed you."

"Better."

He took a step toward her. "I want to kiss you senseless."

She took a step toward him. "I'm listening."

"And make love until we're exhausted."

She laughed. "With two kids who are going to be wearing us out every day, that's not very ambitious."

He put his arms around her waist and she raised his to his neck. "Ah, but those two kids have a grandmother in Atlanta who wants to take them for two weeks in November."

"Sounds like a honeymoon."

He kissed her. "Exactly."

They stared into each other's eyes for several seconds, then his head lowered slowly and he kissed her again. His lips caressed hers with a tenderness that told her a million times over how much he had missed her.

When the kiss ended, he bumped his forehead to hers. "I'm sorry."

"For?"

"For taking so long to think it all through."

"That's okay. That only makes you human."

"You see, that's one of the things I love about you. You let me be me."

She smiled into his eyes. "And you let me be me."

He laughed. There was a light tap at the door and Phil said, "Everything okay in there?"

Mac opened his mouth, but Ellie pressed a finger to his lips. "Let me handle this one." She glanced over Mac's shoulder at the door. "Get lost, Phil."

A loud clearing of Phil's throat let them know he hadn't gotten lost. "Excuse me?"

"You heard the lady. She said, get lost, Phil."

"But—"

Ellie laughed and said, "Go check the perimeter."

"Very good, sir… Um, ma'am."

They waited a few seconds and when Phil didn't say anything else, they broke into gales of laughter.

Mac hugged her and said, "I think you're going to be very good at this."

"There are a lot of other things that I'm actually a lot better at." She pressed a kiss to his neck, then ran her tongue to his ear and whispered a delightful suggestion.

Mac pulled away. "Here? Now?"

The anticipation in his voice made her laugh again. "This might be the one perk of having a live-in nanny and six bodyguards. Not to mention a yard full of friends. I'm pretty sure they can occupy the kids for an hour."

Mac laughed, scooped her off her feet and headed for the master suite.

She stopped him. "I'm guessing one of the guest rooms is prettier than your master suite."

He considered that. "Probably."

"I don't want the first time we make love to be in that ugly red-and-gold thing you call a bedroom."

He changed directions. "Agreed."

Ellie smiled. They did agree. About nearly everything. And disagreed about enough to keep life interesting.

That was the real bottom line. She'd love this guy for the rest of her life because she knew there'd never be a dull moment.

MILLS & BOON®

SEPTEMBER 2010 HARDBACK TITLES

ROMANCE

A Stormy Greek Marriage	Lynne Graham
Unworldly Secretary, Untamed Greek	Kim Lawrence
The Sabbides Secret Baby	Jacqueline Baird
The Undoing of de Luca	Kate Hewitt
Katrakis's Last Mistress	Caitlin Crews
Surrender to Her Spanish Husband	Maggie Cox
Passion, Purity and the Prince	Annie West
For Revenge or Redemption?	Elizabeth Power
Red Wine and Her Sexy Ex	Kate Hardy
Every Girl's Secret Fantasy	Robyn Grady
Cattle Baron Needs a Bride	Margaret Way
Passionate Chef, Ice Queen Boss	Jennie Adams
Sparks Fly with Mr Mayor	Teresa Carpenter
Rescued in a Wedding Dress	Cara Colter
Wedding Date with the Best Man	Melissa McClone
Maid for the Single Dad	Susan Meier
Alessandro and the Cheery Nanny	Amy Andrews
Valentino's Pregnancy Bombshell	Amy Andrews

HISTORICAL

Reawakening Miss Calverley	Sylvia Andrew
The Unmasking of a Lady	Emily May
Captured by the Warrior	Meriel Fuller

MEDICAL™

Dating the Millionaire Doctor	Marion Lennox
A Knight for Nurse Hart	Laura Iding
A Nurse to Tame the Playboy	Maggie Kingsley
Village Midwife, Blushing Bride	Gill Sanderson

SEPTEMBER 2010 LARGE PRINT TITLES

ROMANCE

Virgin on Her Wedding Night	Lynne Graham
Blackwolf's Redemption	Sandra Marton
The Shy Bride	Lucy Monroe
Penniless and Purchased	Julia James
Beauty and the Reclusive Prince	Raye Morgan
Executive: Expecting Tiny Twins	Barbara Hannay
A Wedding at Leopard Tree Lodge	Liz Fielding
Three Times A Bridesmaid...	Nicola Marsh

HISTORICAL

The Viscount's Unconventional Bride	Mary Nichols
Compromising Miss Milton	Michelle Styles
Forbidden Lady	Anne Herries

MEDICAL™

The Doctor's Lost-and-Found Bride	Kate Hardy
Miracle: Marriage Reunited	Anne Fraser
A Mother for Matilda	Amy Andrews
The Boss and Nurse Albright	Lynne Marshall
New Surgeon at Ashvale A&E	Joanna Neil
Desert King, Doctor Daddy	Meredith Webber

MILLS & BOON

OCTOBER 2010 HARDBACK TITLES

ROMANCE

The Reluctant Surrender	Penny Jordan
Shameful Secret, Shotgun Wedding	Sharon Kendrick
The Virgin's Choice	Jennie Lucas
Scandal: Unclaimed Love-Child	Melanie Milburne
Powerful Greek, Housekeeper Wife	Robyn Donald
Hired by Her Husband	Anne McAllister
Snowbound Seduction	Helen Brooks
A Mistake, A Prince and A Pregnancy	Maisey Yates
Champagne with a Celebrity	Kate Hardy
When He was Bad...	Anne Oliver
Accidentally Pregnant!	Rebecca Winters
Star-Crossed Sweethearts	Jackie Braun
A Miracle for His Secret Son	Barbara Hannay
Proud Rancher, Precious Bundle	Donna Alward
Cowgirl Makes Three	Myrna Mackenzie
Secret Prince, Instant Daddy!	Raye Morgan
Officer, Surgeon...Gentleman!	Janice Lynn
Midwife in the Family Way	Fiona McArthur

HISTORICAL

Innocent Courtesan to Adventurer's Bride	Louise Allen
Disgrace and Desire	Sarah Mallory
The Viking's Captive Princess	Michelle Styles

MEDICAL™

Bachelor of the Baby Ward	Meredith Webber
Fairytale on the Children's Ward	Meredith Webber
Playboy Under the Mistletoe	Joanna Neil
Their Marriage Miracle	Sue MacKay

0910 Gen Std LP

MILLS & BOON®

OCTOBER 2010 LARGE PRINT TITLES

ROMANCE

Marriage: To Claim His Twins	Penny Jordan
The Royal Baby Revelation	Sharon Kendrick
Under the Spaniard's Lock and Key	Kim Lawrence
Sweet Surrender with the Millionaire	Helen Brooks
Miracle for the Girl Next Door	Rebecca Winters
Mother of the Bride	Caroline Anderson
What's A Housekeeper To Do?	Jennie Adams
Tipping the Waitress with Diamonds	Nina Harrington

HISTORICAL

Practical Widow to Passionate Mistress	Louise Allen
Major Westhaven's Unwilling Ward	Emily Bascom
Her Banished Lord	Carol Townend

MEDICAL™

The Nurse's Brooding Boss	Laura Iding
Emergency Doctor and Cinderella	Melanie Milburne
City Surgeon, Small Town Miracle	Marion Lennox
Bachelor Dad, Girl Next Door	Sharon Archer
A Baby for the Flying Doctor	Lucy Clark
Nurse, Nanny...Bride!	Alison Roberts